10631933

CODENAME: DANCER

A Dani Spevak Mystery

AMANDA BRICE

Copyright © 2011 Amanda Brice

All rights reserved. No part of this book may be reproduced in any form or by any means without the prior written consent of the author, excepting brief quotes used in reviews.

This is a work of fiction. Names, characters, places, brands, media, and incidents are either the product of the author's imagination or are used fictitiously. The author acknowledges the trademarked status and trademark owners of various products referenced in this work of fiction, which have been used without permission.

For information on the cover design, please contact Amy Lynch Hallenius of Photo Art by Amy (http://www.photoartamy.com).

Cover photograph courtesy of iStockphoto.

ISBN: 1461184010
ISBN-13: 978-1461184010

DEDICATION

*This book is lovingly dedicated to my dear grandmothers,
Helen Spevak San Miguel and Ruth Holmes Sapp.
I love you both so much.*

Praise for *Codename: Dancer*

"Fans of *Pretty Little Liars* and Ally Carter's Gallagher Girls will love *Codename: Dancer*. Sparks fly, tutus twirl, and a clever mystery unravels in what is sure to become a favorite among teens and tweens everywhere. Amanda Brice's debut is a must read for every girl who ever danced – or ever wanted to!"
~ New York Times bestselling author Gemma Halliday

"*Codename Dancer* is a mystery-filled romance that will twirl its way into your heart. Dani is a heroine every girl (and woman) will root for. This is a stand-out debut novel for Amanda Brice!"
~Melissa Francis, author of *Bite Me!* and *Love Sucks!*

"Amanda Brice's debut novel has something that will appeal to everyone, especially ballet enthusiasts, mystery lovers and fans of reality TV competitions. Even if you don't know a thing about dance, you'll be easily drawn into this quick-paced story with authentic characters and big stakes. I adored Dani and found myself rooting for this spunky heroine. Can't wait for the sequel!"
~ Rhonda Stapleton, author of *Struck*

"It reminded me so much of my childhood, and I have no doubt this would have been my favorite series." ~ Broadway actress/dancer Cara Cooper (*Jersey Boys*)

"A perfect example of YA done right."
~ *I'd So Rather Be Reading* review blog

ACKNOWLEGMENTS

A million thanks to authors Gemma Halliday, Gwen Hayes, and Rhonda Stapleton for believing in me. I wouldn't be sharing this story with the world without your encouragement.

To Amy Lynch of Pens and Needles for designing the gorgeous cover gracing the front of this book. I just hope my words are worthy of such a fabulous "costume."

To Lauren Dee of Daisycakes Creative for editing this book and making it ready to be seen by the public.

To Meredith Castile for proofreading on a moment's notice.

To the Fictionistas, Pixie Chicks, Ruby Slippered Sisterhood, and Killer Fiction for all the love and support.

To the Stepmoms for encouraging me to take the publishing plunge and putting up with me when all I wanted to do was talk about my book.

I owe a huge debt to everyone who read this novel in one of its (many!) drafts, especially Emma and Katie Schaefer, Abby Slater, Jeannie Lin, Cynthia Justlin, Jennifer Bianco, and Library Media Specialist Raquell Barton.

Thanks to my niece Daniela for letting me steal her first name for the main character.

To my parents for instilling a lifetime love of reading in me.

But most of all, thanks to my wonderful husband Eric and beautiful daughter Amber. I love you.

CHAPTER 1

My first hint that the devil was wearing Prada earmuffs and a Burberry scarf should've been when my parents gave in and let me go to the Mountain Shadows Academy of the Arts. After all, they'd sworn up and down it would be a cold day in Hades before they let me go away for high school.

I definitely didn't inherit my Grandma Rose's ESP — she's what she calls 'fey' and my dad calls 'crazy' — or I would have realized my world was about to be turned upside down.

But I guess it's not surprising I'd missed the signs. I mean, there's not exactly much use for earmuffs and a scarf in Arizona. I forgot to mention. That's where I would be for the next four years. I was a freshman dance major at Mountain Shadows Academy in Scottsdale, an arts high school founded by Anna Manning Devereaux.

Yes, *that* Anna Devereaux. You may not remember her movies, but I'm sure you've heard of her many marriages. She was this famous starlet in the '50s who made a bunch of old movie musicals with Gene Kelly and Fred Astaire. Anyway, after Hubby Number Eight passed away, she got nostalgic for the Hollywood she once knew and decided to start an arts school to train the next generation. I guess Katy Perry and Snooki didn't exactly inspire much confidence in her.

But Snooki's a novelist, you say. Yeah, and she's read two whole books, too.

When I first moved in, I thought for sure I'd made a huge mistake. My roommate Bev was a complete waste of space. I thought living with an art student would be great. If nothing else, she'd know how to transform the stark white dorm room into something fun and fabulous. Plus she's a sophomore, so she could show me around. But man, was she ever BOR-ING! I wasn't sure she was even capable of answering questions with anything more than one syllable.

I left my friends back home for this?

I plopped down onto my bed and tried to make small talk with the tall girl in black. "So, this is your second year here?"

Bev didn't even turn away from her computer game. "Yes."

"Do you like it?"

"Yeah." She tucked a chunk of dyed black hair behind her ear, revealing more piercings than should be legal.

A root canal would be easier. "And you're an art student?"

"Yes."

I tried another tactic. "The dining hall opens at five?"

She typed furiously for a minute. "Yeah."

"Wanna go?"

"No."

I was stuck with her for the next year. How was I going to make it? I sneaked a peak over her shoulder at the time in the bottom corner of her screen. 4:55. Suddenly, my tummy was growling worse than Chewbaca in a firefight with a couple dozen Imperial Stormtroopers chasing him down.

"Okay, well, see ya later!" I said, grabbing my sunglasses and slipping my feet into my new sparkly black flip-flops. A few seconds later, I was out the door.

I'd wanted to shower and change first — what if I met a really hot guy while standing in the salad bar line? — but I didn't think I'd last much longer in that room without some fresh air. Fortunately I wasn't too sweaty from moving in, and anyway, what were the chances of meeting my soul mate on my first night?

I got my food as quickly as possible, which really wasn't all that quick. The buffet was a thousand times better than the one at Golden Corral, and I'd thought that one was huge! Station after station overflowing with food options tempted me, and I found myself barely able to make a decision.

Yummalicious!

Not that it mattered. I had leotards to fit into, so I had to watch my weight. I placed a salad, bottled water, and a small dish of sugar-free raspberry Jell-O onto my tray, although I eyed the tiramisu.

As I made my way through the crowded room, I noticed all the other kids seemed to be hunched over a flyer. Their whispering permeated the air like my mom's Eternity. Was it an invitation to a super secret party or something? My older sister Whitney told me all about the secret societies at her college. Did we even have that kind of stuff here?

Seeing all the kids huddled together suddenly made me homesick for my old middle school. I never had to worry about where to sit at lunch back at home. We're supposed to eat three meals a day in the caf, but I didn't know anyone, so where was I going to sit?

Deep breath.

Three girls sat at the table in front of me, whispering. Every now and then they looked up from the flyer and scanned the room. Then they laughed and huddled up again. Finally one girl caught my gaze. She had shiny long blonde hair straight out of a shampoo commercial and was wearing a dress suspiciously similar to the one Leighton Meester wore on last night's *Gossip Girl*.

I had to ask where she got it. Not that I could afford it if it was real.

I walked over and placed my tray on the table. "Hi, I'm Dani, can I si—"

The blonde sneered. "You're kidding me, right?"

3

As if on cue, Queen Bee's friends started laughing. All three gathered up their trays and moved to sit with a group of guys at the next table over, occasionally turning back to look at me and laugh.

Did I have something on my shirt? (I was wearing a shirt at least.) Maybe I wasn't wearing the right one. Or even worse, maybe a huge zit erupted on my nose?

I was surrounded by a sea of people, bobbing along on the waves and forced to sink or swim. What would it be? I clutched my tray just like a life raft.

I'd never felt so alone. So small.

So … nothing.

I considered bringing dinner back to Ames Hall to eat in my room — even spending time with Bev had to be better than letting everyone think I was a loser who ate alone — when I saw a tall girl wearing a pink tank top with rhinestones across the chest waving in my direction.

For a second there I thought she meant someone else, but apparently not, because she strode over to me. "Don't let them bother you. They just think they're too cool for school. Whatev. You're the new freshman in Bev's room, right?" When I nodded, she stuck her hand out for me to shake. "I'm Maya."

My hands were full holding my tray, so I did an elaborate balancing act with one hand and my hip and stuck out my right hand. "Dani."

Maya motioned for me to follow her to where she was sitting with a group of guys and girls. "What program are you in?"

"Dance." Wow. I was about as talkative as my goth-girl roommate. What was wrong with me?

"Me too." Maya's cocoa-colored eyes shone. "So, what do you think of Bev?"

"Uh—" I stammered.

She held up a finger to silence me. "Don't worry. I don't like her either. She hates dancers. Total freak show."

We finally approached Maya's friends' table. They, too, were huddled over a colorful flyer.

"Hey," Maya said and caught their attention. "This is Dani. She lives with Bev Marcus." The kids shot me a sympathetic

4

look. "Dani, everyone." Maya plopped herself down in between a short Hispanic girl and a guy who quite frankly put the Sparta boys to shame. Whoa.

Hmm ... looked like I was gonna like it here!

I placed my tray down at the empty spot next to a cute guy with spiky blond hair, dressed in a black T-shirt and ripped jeans. "What's that?" I pointed at the flyer.

The Hispanic girl pushed the piece of paper over to me. "They chose our school for the next season of *Teen Celebrity Dance-off*!"

"It's not fair that the auditions are only open to dance students," Blond Spiky Boy said. "And let me guess, Analisa won't be auditioning anyway because it'll take away from your serious dance career?"

"Well, yes, it's not ballet. That's true," the Hispanic girl said. "But as long as we still make our regular classes and rehearsals, it could only help."

"So you are gonna try out?"

"Whatever, Kyle. You know you can't dance anyway," Maya said, dismissing him with her hand.

"Ladies, aren't you going to introduce me to your friend?" A tall guy with dark brown hair and piercing blue eyes the color of the Caribbean extended his hand and let it linger. Contacts? Had to be. Nobody had eyes that blue naturally. "Hi, I'm Craig," he said, smiling and revealing the most adorable set of dimples I'd ever seen. He looked like he walked straight out of the pages of the Abercrombie catalog. Since Mountain Shadows didn't teach modeling, I guessed 'actor.'

"Dani," I squeaked.

I was forced to rethink my decision not to shower. I mentally cursed myself for being anxious to get away from Bev.

Maya smacked Craig's hand away as if he were a mosquito. "Don't let him bother you."

"He's not bothering me."

Maya sighed. "Whatever. I wanna hear more about the show."

What were the chances I'd get on, especially against the senior girls? But still, I had a shot. Maybe not a good one, since my training was mostly limited to the classics, but I could still try. Man, this school was so cool. Much better than Sparta High.

"Who's on the show?" I asked.

Analisa consulted the flyer. "So far, they've confirmed Daronn Williams, and John Michael Cooper, but rumor has it Prince Harry and Daniel Radcliffe are in negotiations."

I giggled. "Prince Harry and Harry Potter?"

Analisa cleared her throat before continuing. "Well, I seriously doubt the prince will do it. Isn't he in the Royal Marines or something? Personally, I'm hoping for Robert Pattinson."

"Yeah, right." Maya's laughter sounded more like a snort. "Like he'd really do this. I think that's illegal anyway. He'd have to dance with underage girls."

Wow, all those stars were totally hot. Daronn's debut hip-hop CD landed him at the top of the Billboards at just sixteen, and who wasn't in love with JMC?

"Just guys?" I asked.

Analisa tossed back her curls. "Looks that way. I recognize most of them, but not Michael Cooper."

I laughed. "You mean John Michael Cooper, right?"

Analisa blushed. "Oops, right."

"You don't know who JMC is?"

Analisa shrugged, twirling a strand of fettuccine with her fork. She wasn't worried about carbs?

"Um, Great Expectations? Hello?" I asked.

"The book?"

Kyle rolled his eyes. "The band. They're all over MTV."

"Sorry, but I was never really allowed to listen to popular music," Analisa explained. "My mom's a ballet teacher. I only listened to music by dead white guys growing up."

Maya shook her head slowly and whistled. "Girl, that's some warped life you led."

I felt my forehead scrunch up as I thought. "Why aren't there any girls?"

"They were hoping to get Miley Cyrus and Taylor Swift, but there was this whole controversy about whether Miley was a good role model and Taylor was too expensive," Kyle explained.

"Anyway, their target demographic is teenage girls, so it just makes sense to only have guy stars," Analisa said.

"Taylor Swift, now that's a chick I could get behind." A smirk graced Craig's well-chiseled face.

Maya turned towards him, exasperation darkening her expression. "Was anyone talking to you? I didn't think so."

"So, how's it work?" I asked.

A third guy, a tall, skinny Asian kid who, up to now, had been quietly doodling anime figures in his sketch pad, said, "They're gonna choose five dance students to be partners for the stars. But I really don't think it's fair that only dance students can audition."

"What do you care whether it's just dancers?" Maya asked.

"Because," Craig answered slowly, dragging out his syllables, spelling it out as if for a bunch of infants. "It's national TV. My big break." His already incredible eyes flashed a bright, piercing blue, making me go weak in the knees. It was a good thing I was sitting.

Definitely an aspiring actor.

Analisa laughed. "They're only choosing girls."

"That's just it," Ryan said. "It's discrimination. We should sue."

"Big words." Maya smirked. "Someone's been reading his Constitution, huh?"

I cleared my throat. "Actually, I think it's only discrimination if the government does it. So you can't sue." Everyone stared at me like I'd grown a second head. "My mom's a law professor."

Craig smiled in my direction. "Guess we better listen to the new girl."

Kyle fixed a hard stare on me. "I'm sure we could still sue."

Maya shook her head and rolled her eyes. "Whatev. You trying out for *Law & Order: Special High School Unit*? Cut the act." She stood up, lifting her tray with the regal air of a queen dismissing her subjects. "Gentlemen, it's been real, but my girls and I gotta finish eating and get practicing."

She marched away, and we followed her to a nearby table. I kept sneaking looks back at Craig and his friends, though.

"Why did we leave?" I asked. "They seemed really fun."

"Tim's pretty cool. Kyle has his moments," Analisa admitted. "But Craig is a total jerk."

I looked over my shoulder at the guys we'd just left sitting a few tables away. Craig definitely looked like the leader of the pack. "He seems pretty nice."

Actually, he seemed really hot, but I wasn't going to admit that to the girls just yet. Not when I barely even knew them. I'd start with nice. Nice was neutral. Nice was safe.

I could deal with nice.

"Girl, everyone in school thinks that, and it goes straight to his head," Maya told me, a conspiratorial tone coloring her words. "Really arrogant. I don't fall for that shit."

"Yeah, don't get any ideas. Everyone wants to date him," Analisa said. "Anyway, I think he's still with Hadley Taylor."

"Who's Hadley Taylor?"

Maya gestured over her shoulder. "You just met her."

Great.

"He probably only likes her because she's totally rich. One of the upper class girls' dorms is named after her dad," Maya continued. "Plus, she's a junior and danced Sugar Plum her sophomore year."

Shoot. Hadley Taylor was serious competition. Nobody ever got the role of the Sugar Plum Fairy that young. I was way out of my league. Better write Craig off.

I knew I wouldn't meet the guy of my dreams tonight.

"What grade are they in?" I asked, motioning towards the table of guys.

"Seniors," Maya and Analisa answered at the same time.

"Craig has an audition for the Yale Drama Program in two weeks, but it's just a formality," Analisa said. "Everyone knows he's going there."

"And if not there, then either UCLA or Northwestern." Maya shrugged. "He's a cocky jerk, but damn, the boy can act."

I looked back at the other table. "So how do we try out?"

CHAPTER 2

It seemed like auditions couldn't possibly arrive soon enough. The first two weeks of school, which normally were a whirlwind of emotions and excitement anyway, were transformed into a mad rush to rehearse.

Okay, so it probably wasn't the greatest idea ever to skip math homework and spend more time at the studio, but, well, priorities, you know? I mean, would I ever need to prove two triangles similar in the real world? Seriously? On the other hand, the show could be the big break in my dance career. Ballroom might not have much in common with ballet, but I came to this school to perform, not crunch numbers in my calculator.

Had I been at home, there was no way Mom and Dad would've let me get away with not doing geometry, but they weren't here, and what they didn't know couldn't possibly hurt them.

What happened at boarding school stayed at boarding school.

I broke up the monotony of the rehearsal schedule with a coffee date with Craig on Saturday afternoon – go me! Guess he didn't like Hadley Taylor after all.

I drummed my nails on the table at Starbucks as I waited. Fellow students flitted in and out as they satisfied their caffeine cravings.

Good thing I had my cell phone, because I was there for-freaking-ever. Plenty of time to text my friends back home, but it sucked I still had my lame old skool cell. It didn't have a QWERTY keyboard, so I had to hit the dialing keys the exact right number of times to register each letter. Blech. Only good thing was that it took three times as long to type out a text, so it killed the extra time pretty well.

Hadley Taylor had an iPhone. I hated her.

The door chimes twinkled the entrance of a new person at least fifty times. Every time they rang, my head snapped up to see if it was Craig. I was nursing a crick in my neck from a particularly strenuous workout that morning, and my near-stalking of the door didn't exactly help to relieve my aching muscles.

I must have seen the entire school at some point that afternoon, but not the one I wanted to see.

Can you believe it? He stood me up! Maybe he was still dating Hadley. But if so, then why did he ask me out?

Whatever. Maya was right. I didn't need him. And I definitely didn't need the calories from a double mocha either.

I had bigger plans.

By Friday, the day of the audition, the producers had settled on a celebrity cast. Turned out Harry Potter and Prince Harry weren't available, and neither was Robert Pattinson, so they filled the remaining spots with Carson Chen, a seventeen-year-old tennis phenom who gave Roger Federer a run for his money earlier this summer, and Nick Galliano, an up-and-coming teen actor who's had several roles in big movies. You probably don't know the name, but you'd recognize the face. And, boy, what a face. He epitomizes the cliché of tall, dark, and handsome and makes Craig look average.

Believe me, that's darn near impossible.

Four guys. Which meant only one thing. Just four spots for Mountain Shadows girls. What were the chances I'd get in? I mean, I was only a freshman. There were about fifty upper-class girls with much more dance training.

But that didn't mean I wasn't going to try. Work hard, play hard.

In order to make up for lost time, I spent pretty much all my waking hours at the studio, morning, noon, and night. I took all the extra dance classes I could and then continued to practice when there weren't any lessons. I didn't even snack. Normally, I was a closet Hershey's addict, but I just couldn't risk it. I could not gain weight.

I had a sneaking suspicion looks were more important than talent in this audition. After all, we'd be on TV for the whole world to see.

Why couldn't I have Whitney's boobs?

I was scheduled to try out at one, so I didn't arrive to the audition until 12:50. Instead, I warmed up at one of the practice studios nearby because I didn't want to be surrounded by girls freaking out. Who needed that kind of tension? It's hard enough to focus on auditions without the distraction of dancers in the full throes of a nervous breakdown worthy of a Black Swan diva.

No thank you.

"Daniela Spevak?"

Now or never.

I crept onstage and took my opening pose. As the music filled the auditorium, I knew I had to hit it. I chose to do a contemporary pointe routine because pretty much everyone else was doing hip hop or pop — styles that looked more in place on MTV — but I wanted to stand out. Besides, I'm not the best at booty-poppin', so I figured I'd have a better chance if I showcased my classical technique.

I opened slowly with some *boureés*, trying my best to keep the sound of my toe shoes clacking on the floor to a minimum. I know Pavlova's *boureés* were no louder than a whisper, but today mine sounded more like a herd of elephants clomping through the jungle. Or maybe a pack of football players running to the end zone, fully suited up in heavy pads and equipment.

Oh my Gawd. There was no way I'd get on the show now unless I got my butt in gear. And quick!

I turned to the back of the stage out of view of the judges. *Breathe in, breathe out.* I couldn't exactly lie on the floor, but maybe the yoga breathing would help?

Wrong. My timing got all screwed up, and I stumbled and fell off pointe. Just as I was about to give up, something caught my eye waiting in the wings. Or rather, someone.

Craig. Just standing there alone, leaning against the wall with his arms crossed.

How dare he show up here after standing me up last weekend? Well, I'd show him. I just had to make it into the cast.

Talk about motivation. I moved effortlessly into a series of *chaîné* turns and then into a *petit allegro*, complete with as many jumps as possible. Then the music slowed down and with it, my steps, in the *adagio* portion of the piece. I let my body melt into the luxurious tune and became one with the music. I didn't even look at the audience, but just danced for the sheer joy of it.

Finally, I ended with my signature — sixteen *fouettés*, whipping my leg out to gain momentum in my turn. One of these days I'd be able to work my way up to thirty-two in a row, but not today. Today, I was lucky to just hit these!

After the piece, I caught my breath while basking in the infectious roar of the applause. I ran backstage to strip off my toe shoes and grab a drink of water. My next routine would be barefoot, a contemporary Afro-Cuban rhythm, and I needed all the strength I could get.

As the electrifying first drum beats pounded, I leapt across the stage and twirled and twirled and threw my body into incomprehensible positions as I let myself get carried away by the hypnotic beat. In fact, I totally forgot my choreographed routine and began improvising, just dancing my little heart out.

I finally channeled all my pent-up frustration and energy and let it come roaring out in my dance. I honestly didn't know who that girl was up onstage. She certainly didn't resemble the Dani who'd auditioned for arts school just five months earlier. And she definitely wasn't a product of Miss Michelle's.

In a word, I rocked.

The auditorium burst into the loudest applause I'd ever heard in my brief dance career. Trust me, I'd never get enough of that sound! When it subsided, an extremely proper-sounding male British voice called out from the dark, "Miss Spevak, is it? Could you please come back at three? You've made it to the next round."

Sweet!

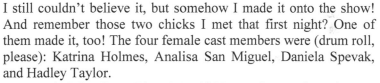

I still couldn't believe it, but somehow I made it onto the show! And remember those two chicks I met that first night? One of them made it, too! The four female cast members were (drum roll, please): Katrina Holmes, Analisa San Miguel, Daniela Spevak, and Hadley Taylor.

Yeah, Miss Sugar Plum herself. Not too happy about that.

But who cares? It's not like I really knew her anyway. So what if she was Craig's girlfriend? It just didn't matter. I was gonna be on TV!

Even better, I was going to dance with Nick Galliano. Nick Galliano! Can you believe it? He's way hotter than Craig anyway. Okay, so he's not as well-known as JMC, but he was going to be huge someday. And maybe he'd have me to thank for it. I could just picture it, him accepting his Oscar:

> *"I'd like to thank Daniela Spevak for being the
> best dance partner ever. I love you!"*

Yeah, boarding school was the best decision my parents ever made.

Speaking of my parents, I felt a twinge of guilt at not calling to tell them the good news, but I was due on the set for a "get-to-know-you" event. Now that we were on the show, we had to actually look comfortable dancing with our partners, not like a bunch of star-struck teenyboppers oohing and ahhing over their every move.

Riiight.

I arrived at the set in time to hear the executive producer, Brooks Hawkins, ask us to introduce ourselves. He caught me sneaking in late and told me to go first.

A flush of warmth came over me as I did my very best impression of a stop sign. You know, the color? "Uh, I'm Dani."

He peered at me over the top of his half-glasses, a crease forming in his forehead, like he didn't quite know what to make of me. He must have been satisfied, though, because he motioned for me to join the others in the circle. "What else?" he asked in a very clipped, very British accent.

What else? Uh ... "I'm from Sparta, New Jersey." What was with the Minnie Mouse squeak? "My favorite style is pointe, but I also love contemporary. Um, I'm a freshman."

"And your last name?"

I blushed again and scooched in between Nick and a cute redhead. "Sorry. Spevak."

Mr. Hawkins sighed, clearly annoyed at having to make like a dentist and pull teeth. Nothing like the great first impression I was making. *Whoo-hoo, Dani! Way to go.* "And you're dancing, with?"

Not quite as bad as Simon Cowell, but the accent definitely didn't help to put me at ease. I giggled nervously. "Sorry. I'm dancing with Nick."

I was embarrassed to have Nick see me acting like such an idiot. I wanted to find the nearest hole and crawl into it for the next four years. Come out and join the human race when I was a respectable eighteen, like my big sister, Whit. She'd never act like a giggly schoolgirl.

But amazingly, Nick seemed completely oblivious to my dumbassness. I snuck a peak at him out of the corner of my eye and he just smiled, which made his warm brown eyes look just like melted chocolate and totally put me at ease.

A movie star smiled at me.

Oh. My. God. A movie star smiled at me!

And not just any movie star, but only the best-looking one on the whole planet. He could choose just about any starlet in the entire English-speaking world, heck, even in the non-English-speaking world, and yet he smiled at me.

Me!

This type of thing never happened in Sparta!

I began daydreaming about our future wedding and was so

wrapped up in planning out every second of our next seventy-five-ish years I completely missed the rest of the introductions. But not for long.

Just as Hadley Taylor was going on and on, flipping her perfectly waved blond hair back and forth, back and forth, over her shoulders, and telling everyone, *um, like, you know, like,* her whole life story, we heard a loud crash.

Okay, so "crash" didn't exactly do justice to what we heard. Way too calm. This sounded more like a couple hundred pounds of theatre background set hurtling to the ground at breakneck speed.

Which was exactly what it was.

Everyone jumped up, leaving Hadley to babble almost incoherently to herself, and dashed backstage to see what happened.

"What is it?"

"Who designed this piece of crap, anyway?"

"Are you sure everyone's okay?"

That's when we realized it. Apparently not everyone was okay. I was so wrapped up in my daydream I never even noticed the redhead chick, Kat Holmes, excuse herself to go to the restroom. Only she never made it there.

Because she was lying on the floor, not moving.

"Call 911!" Mr. Hawkins yelled. His assistant, Tracy, pulled out her cell phone and started dialing.

Nobody said a word while we waited for the paramedics. Kat was breathing, but she wasn't responding. I'd never seen an unconscious person before. Not even when Whitney fell off Renata Ricci's shoulders during the cheerleading routine at the halftime of the basketball state finals and her spotter just jumped out of the way instead of catching her. Whit had blacked out for a moment, but she'd already come to by the time my parents and I got to her.

But not Kat. She was just ... lying there. Freaked me out.

After the EMTs took Kat away on a stretcher, you could almost hear a pin drop in the theatre. If the others were thinking what I was, they were glad it didn't happen to them but felt kinda guilty it had to happen to someone.

A sheepish-looking stagehand appeared out of nowhere, his shoulders slumping and head hanging. "I checked every inch of the set just this afternoon, and it was fine." He shook his head, longish sandy blond hair flapping over his eyes. "Everything was in place. I just don't understand how this could have happened."

"You!" Mr. Hawkins barked at the stagehand. "What's your name?"

"Steve ... "

"Well, Steven, what happened?"

His embarrassment turned to despair. "I don't know what happened. Like I said, I checked everything fully this afternoon, and I'm sure Marc checked it also, this evening before he left."

The producer narrowed his already beady eyes. "Well, Steven, we absolutely cannot have this happening again. This is a very important show, and we have some very important guests here." He gestured at the stars standing behind him. "I cannot risk any more injuries to anyone."

"More like he can't risk any lawsuits," Analisa whispered.

Wasn't that the truth? A lawsuit from any one of the celebrities could bankrupt *Teen Celebrity Dance-Off*. And that would definitely mean the end of my fifteen minutes of fame before age fifteen.

Mr. Hawkins spun to face the crowd of dancers and stars gathered around him. "We are on a very tight schedule here. We simply cannot have any more disruptions. It's bad enough we have to work around your school—" he sneered "—work, but I can't allow any drama concerning the set and the stagehands to throw us off." He pivoted on his heel and spun around to face the helpless stagehand. "Steven, I suggest you pay better attention to your handiwork in the future."

"I swear—" Steve began.

"I don't need any excuses!" Mr. Hawkins snapped. His face contorted into a mask of hatred that would be perfect for the drama department. "A girl is in the hospital! If you cannot do your job properly and ensure the sets are changed without causing any more incidents or injury to the cast then I'll find someone who can."

A chilling silence fell over the room like a thick velvet stage curtain. I glanced at my cast mates and if the expressions on their faces were any indication, nobody knew what to say. Poor Steve. I didn't even know the guy, but Mr. Hawkins was being really mean. It was an accident! Couldn't he see that?

Mr. Hawkins marched briskly across the stage, down the stairs into the audience, and turned towards the nearest exit. He paused with his hand on the door and turned around to face us again.

"Rehearsals begin tomorrow. Your schedules, which list your dance styles, are being delivered to your rooms right now. Please be on time. I don't need to explain how unhappy I would be if anyone was late, do I?"

CHAPTER 3

The next day was Saturday, so fortunately we didn't have any academic or dance classes. But that didn't mean we didn't have any work to do. Even under normal conditions — you know, when you're not in the cast of a major television program — Saturdays at the Mountain Shadows Academy mean rehearsals, rehearsals, and more rehearsals.

And then some more rehearsals.

When I had arrived back to my room the night before, I found my schedule and discovered that Nick Galliano and I would be learning a cha-cha. We were supposed to meet in Studio B at ten in the morning for a two-hour choreography session and then spend the rest of the day practicing. Dance, dance, dance. My kind of day!

With all the excitement of the day's events, my suitemates and I (well, not Bev) were up most of the night talking, so I totally overslept Saturday morning. As great as it was to be away at school with no parents, I had to admit that my mom yelling at me to get up was way better than any alarm clock could ever be. This whole "responsibility" thing was going to take some getting used to.

"Morning, sunshine."

I strained to open my eyes one at a time, blinking as bright sunlight nearly blinded me. I didn't remember leaving my blinds open. What the ... ?

"Wake up, Sleeping Beauty," Maya said. The taller girl towered over my prone position with a big grin on her face. Maybe she'd take my mom's place and threaten to pour water over my head if I didn't get out of bed.

"How did you get in here?" I asked.

"Simple. Your door was unlocked."

Mental forehead smack. "What time is it?" I groaned.

"Nine-forty-five. You've got exactly fifteen minutes to drag your sorry butt outta bed, to the dining hall to grab a bagel, and off to the studio."

I squinted at the red digital numbers on my clock. It couldn't really be ... Yikes it was!

"Why do I need to go to the dining hall?"

She stared at me like I was crazy. "Um, the most important meal of the day?"

"Wait a sec," I said, rubbing the sleep from my eyes. "How do you know the schedule?"

Maya plopped down on the corner of my bed. "I'm in the show."

That got my attention. "How?"

"Don't be so shocked, Dani." Maya feigned an expression of hurt. Or maybe she really was. I was still half asleep after all. "I'm actually a pretty damn good dancer, you know."

I sat up straight. "Well, duh. You wouldn't be here if you weren't."

"Kat's in the hospital with a concussion, and they don't know when she'll be able to dance again. So Mr. Hawkins took her out of the show because they can't afford to push back the premiere, and I'm taking her place."

"Oh my gosh! That's so cool!" I stopped myself from jumping up and giving her a big hug when I realized how callous that sounded about Kat. "I mean, that stinks for Kat and all, but it's lucky for you. I'm so excited!"

I was running really late, so I just pulled on any old leotard and tights, grabbed my dance bag, and sprinted across campus to the dance building. I didn't need a shower; I'd be sweating soon enough anyway. And I definitely didn't have time to grab breakfast. Besides, I had costumes to fit into, so it might actually help.

Crap. I was late to my first choreography session. Just by five minutes, mind you, but it was more than enough to earn me a rather proper British 'talking to' from Mr. Hawkins. *Mental note: don't piss Simon Cowell off.*

Yes, I know Simon Cowell was much more charming than this guy.

I'd never taken a cha-cha class before, and it was surprisingly difficult. I'd always been really good at all styles of dance, but for some reason, I had problems with partnering. Maybe it was me. Or maybe it was Nick. He might be hot, but he wasn't exactly the world's greatest dancer.

I'm not sure what it was, but although we had this totally amazing connection — I knew he could look into my soul and see how beautiful I was, both inside and out, even though I'd lost the gene pool boob lottery — we had a hard time showing it on the dance floor. Okay, so I'm sure it didn't help that every time he took my hand in his a thousand volts of energy surged through my body, making me go completely weak in the knees. Knee problems weren't exactly the greatest when your partner was spinning you like the teacups at Disney World and twisting your body into nearly impossible positions that would even impress the Cirque du Soleil gymnasts.

Finally, after what felt like about a million years, but was really less than two hours, the choreographers told us that they had to move on to the next couple, and we were on our own.

Which meant only one thing. I was left alone in Studio B with Nick Galliano. A girl's imagination could go wild.

Thanks, Mom and Dad, for this whole boarding school thing!

If my BFF had been there, I would've been jumping up and

down, bouncing off the walls, squeeing like a little girl. But she was back in Sparta, and I wasn't about to squee by myself. Especially not in front of my future husband. How embarrassing!

"So, Dani," Nick said, snapping me out of my daydream. "What's there to do for fun around here?"

"Uh," I began. Why do I always clam up around hot guys? "I don't really know." I giggled nervously. "I just got here."

"Well, then would you be interested in having dinner with me tonight?" He flashed me a thousand watt smile that just lit up the room. If Mountain Shadows wanted to cut energy costs, they should keep him around. "We can discover what there is to do in this city, together."

Was I still daydreaming, or did Nick Galliano just ask me out on a date? Or was he just being nice? Dinner on a Saturday night. That's a date, right?

Ohmygoshohmygoshohmygosh! My first real date ever would be with a movie star! The kids back home in Sparta would never believe this!

Heck, I couldn't even believe it!

I couldn't wait to call my sister at college. I knew there was no way she could possibly beat this gossip.

After that, I was pretty much a goner. Concentration, what's that? I know it's a cliché, but I spent the rest of the rehearsal just walking on air. I was pretty sure someone would have to scrape me off the ceiling or I would never return to Earth. And who'd want to?

Reality was way overrated.

After another hour or so of practicing (or rather, trying to practice but failing miserably), Nick suggested that we take a break and find something to eat.

I scooped up my dance bag and trotted behind him like a love struck little puppy into the lobby. I knew I was acting like an idiot. I could hear Whitney's voice in my head: *Act natural, Dani. And whatever you do, don't let him know you're interested.*

"So, what'll it be?" Again, that smile. He was killing me. "Reese's or Snickers?"

"Neither. I'm allergic to peanuts."

"Man, that sucks." His brown eyes flooded with concern.

Could he be any more perfect? Sensitive, in touch with his feelings, and looked like a male model! "Okay, Lays or Doritos?"

I couldn't exactly eat either of those options, considering I had costumes to fit into, but I didn't want him to think I was a prissy little girly-girl. My mom always told me that guys like girls who eat.

I could do some crunches later, right? A hundred ought to do it. A hundred before dinner, I mean. There was still time for more tonight.

"Doritos." I shot him my most charming smile, hoping that if he was dazzled by my looks he might not notice my lack of a chest. "And a Diet Coke, please."

Nick popped some coins into the machine. Out spit the snacks. He tossed me a bag of chips as though it was a football, ripped open his own bag, and plopped himself down on a couch, stretching out his long legs. I felt silly standing there while he lounged, so I joined him on the couch.

"So ... " I didn't know what to say. "Fun session, huh?"

He shoved a handful of potato chips in his mouth and crunched down loudly. "I guess it was okay."

"Yeah, you're right. It wasn't that great." *Shut up, Dani. You're not even making any sense.*

He poured the crumbs from the bottom of the bag into his mouth, then popped up like one of those Whack-a-Moles in the game tent at the county fair and bought two more bags.

All right, what now?

I felt really cold all of a sudden, so I grabbed a sweater out of my bag.

"The McCauleys seem pretty nice." Not exactly the brilliant conversational starter I was looking for, but it would do.

"Who?"

"The McCauleys." I reached into my dance bag, pulled out my shoe brush, and raked it across the suede bottoms of my dance shoes. "They choreographed the routine."

"Yeah, they're okay."

Silence.

"We're pretty lucky to get them. They won at Blackpool last year."

His face was as expressionless as a mind-controlled assassin. He clearly had no idea what I was talking about. "It's a really big competition — never mind."

I concentrated on brushing the bottoms of my shoes to fill the time. If he wasn't going to talk, then I'd at least do something productive. Dancing mattes the suede down and makes your soles slippery. You need to rake a metal brush over them to rough up the soles so you have traction. This task lasted for all of about a minute before I tried again in vain to make chitchat.

"So, that was weird about the set last night, huh?"

Nick looked up sharply. "What about it?"

"Uh, I don't know. It was just weird."

He shot me a strange look. "Yeah."

I waited for him to elaborate, but nothing. Okay, then. I pictured us twenty years from now, hanging out in our living room not saying anything to each other. Might need to rethink those wedding plans.

But that thought vanished as soon as he flashed another of his famous smiles. Yeah, I could totally marry him. Not like tomorrow or anything – I'm only fourteen, and I don't live in a backwards Third World country. But, I don't know. Like in ten years.

Who needs conversation?

He downed his soda, crushed the can in his hand, and turned to me. "Wanna go back in there?"

"Okay!" I said, way too eagerly.

Once back in the studio, Nick turned the music on so we could go through the routine again. I guess the snack break did the trick, though, because it was the best time yet.

I started with my back to the audience, and then walked around Nick. He spun me in then opened out to a parallel position just as the music heated up.

We hit every move just the way the McCauleys taught us. We even got all the lifts without falling, which was a good thing, because I was turning black and blue under my dance clothes from all our previous mishaps. About freaking time we got it right.

At the end of the routine, Nick lowered me into a dip and we locked eyes. But instead of breaking away so we could take our bows, he held the pose for longer than I expected. Much longer. In fact, he seemed to be leaning in even closer. My heart started beating wildly, like it did during the ice breaker session the night before. The connection was so intense, I just knew this was the moment I'd been waiting for. He was going to kiss me.

I closed my eyes, anticipating —

"Bomb! Everyone get out of the building! Now!"

It wasn't exactly the amazing, romantic experience I'd been hoping for. In fact, Nick dropped me as he sprung up, and I fell hard on the floor for about the hundredth time that morning. And Mr. Hearts and Flowers didn't wait for me, either, as he ran out the door to find the source of the commotion.

I picked myself off the floor and rushed into the lobby. Mr. Hawkins' assistant, Tracy, screamed, "Bomb! Bomb!" at the top of her lungs just a second or two before a shrill, ear-piercing alarm erupted. It continued to go off at equal two-second intervals, eliminating any conceivable possibility that anyone could ignore it.

Why would anybody bomb our school?

But I wasn't going to just stand there waiting for an answer. I had to get out of there! And besides, I didn't really have a choice. Teachers appeared as if out of nowhere, herding us like cattle to the exits. I ran after the other dancers and stars as everyone attempted to push their way out.

Once outside, we kept running until we reached the main quad of the campus, where we practically fell over one another, hugging like one big happy family, just thankful we'd gotten out. What would've happened if we didn't?

Why did the producers think there was a bomb in the building? What did they see?

"Dude, this sucks!" hip-hop artist Daronn said.

"I know!" said Carson, the tennis player. "We could've been killed."

"Who found it?" Maya asked.

"I think Tracy found it." Analisa hugged her arms against her chest. "Scary stuff."

"Apparently she heard a ticking noise," Carson said.

"Yeah," JMC, boy bander extraordinaire, said. "Hadley and I heard it too, didn't we?" He glanced towards his partner.

Hadley twirled a long, silky blond strand of hair around the palm of her hand, strangely silent for once. "It was really scary," she finally answered, her eyes completely devoid of any normal expression or reaction. "Just this tick-tick-tick, like some kind of timer or something."

Everybody got really quiet after that, as though we were expecting to hear the natural result of that tick-tick-tick at any moment.

Only we didn't.

A siren pierced through the eerie midday silence, alerting us to the arrival of the bomb squad. Sure enough, within moments, an alphabet soup of men in dark windbreakers emblazoned with three capital letters on the back swarmed the dance studio. I couldn't exactly make out the initials from all the way across the quad – maybe ATF or FBI? Probably both. Who knew what agencies were there?

We all exchanged glances, nobody wanting to ruin the ability to eavesdrop on any new information that we might catch. But the studio was too far away, so eventually we gave up and tried in vain to pretend nothing was wrong. We continued to make awkward chitchat for the next half hour, but nobody's heart was in it. There was only one thing on anyone's mind.

As I looked in the direction of the soon-to-explode dance studio, I spotted the producer, Mr. Hawkins, approaching our little gathering place. He had a really pissed-off expression on his face, like he'd just sat on a cactus. His assistant Tracy trailed after him, struggling to keep up with his brisk pace.

"Ladies and gentleman," he announced in his perfectly clipped voice. "We have some good news and some bad news." He looked expectantly at his assistant.

"Good news first," Daronn said.

Tracy cleared her throat before she began. "The bomb squad has determined it was a false alarm."

"That's great!" I squealed. "So we're all safe?"

Tracy scuffed the toe of her shiny black pump in the grass. "Well, not exactly. The fact remains that someone rigged a fake bomb, with nails, complete with wires, and a timer, inside a pipe, to make it look like there was actually a bomb in the building."

"Who would do that?" Analisa asked.

Mr. Hawkins stared straight at me. "Who indeed?"

Tracy cleared her throat, visibly uncomfortable. "That's what the police are going to figure out."

"Any suspects?" Nick asked.

"Um, actually, I'm not sure we should discuss it, but, well, the bomb was found in Daniela's dance bag." Tracy looked away as she spoke.

"Well, Miss Spevak?" Mr. Hawkins peered at me over the top of his half-rimmed spectacles. "Do you have anything to say for yourself?"

Hindsight is 20/20, and I now know it was completely unprofessional of me, but apparently my foresight was in desperate need of glasses. "The show must go on?"

CHAPTER 4

If I'd known I was going to spend the first afternoon of my television career giving statements down at the police station, I don't know if I would have auditioned. How was I improving my craft if I couldn't practice? And this was taking me away from the studio.

Oh, who am I kidding? Of course I would have.

But seriously, even though they spoke to everyone in the cast, they spent the most time with little ol' me. Gee thanks. Apparently they seemed to think that just because the bomb was in my bag that I'd know something about it. Did I really look like the type of girl who knew how to build a bomb?

Even a fake one?

Speaking of fake, I didn't like to gossip, but Maya told me that Hadley Taylor came back after Christmas break last year with bigger boobs. Can you believe it? She's sixteen. Sheesh.

Hmm, I wonder if my parents would go for it?

"So you say you were with Mr. Galliano all afternoon, Miss

Spevak?"

Didn't I just say so? Okay, so I didn't say that out loud. That would be stupid. But as my lawyer mom would say, "asked and answered, dude." (Fine, she doesn't say "dude.") I swear I was repeating myself for the gazillionth time as I said, "Yes, we were practicing in Studio B."

The blond cop flipped through his notepad. "And you say that you were practicing for a TV show?"

His voice had a really skeptical edge to it. I admit that it's not every day that a high school girl appears on TV, but this is a performers' school. Our founder was a former Hollywood starlet, after all.

Back in the dorm later that afternoon, the fake bomb was all anyone could talk about. The news spread like kudzu in the Carolinas. And unfortunately, if the conversations I'd overheard in the hall bathroom were any indication, apparently everyone thought I was to blame.

Okay, I lied. Some people thought Maya did it.

But for some weird reason, Maya and Analisa believed me.

"No way, Dani," Maya said. "That's crazy talk."

Analisa nodded. "Anyone can tell how excited you are." She squeezed my hand. "There's no way you'd do anything to jeopardize being on the show."

"It just doesn't make any sense," Maya said, staring out the window in the direction of the dance studio. "Why would anyone do it?"

I lay down on the floor and tried to stretch myself out further than my full five-foot-three, hoping to channel my energy like we'd been taught in yoga. "Why me?"

Analisa plopped down beside me and immediately twisted herself into a complicated yoga pose that I'd never seen before. "I wouldn't worry about it. It's a stupid practical joke. Someone's just jealous."

I shook my head, a difficult task considering I was supposed to lie completely still. "I'm not so sure."

"What do you mean?" Analisa asked.

I sat up, abandoning the relaxation technique. What the heck, it's not like it was working anyway. "I don't know. But the set flat did fall last night and hurt Kat."

"But that was just an accident," Analisa said.

"Maybe not," Maya said, walking to the center of the room and joining us on the floor. "You know, maybe Dani's right. Someone might be trying to sabotage the show."

"But who?" I asked.

Analisa scrunched her forehead while she thought. "Someone who's jealous?"

"Or who doesn't want the show to go on," Maya said.

"No way, everyone wants the show to go on!" I said. "It's the most exciting thing that's ever happened here."

"Well, not exactly," Maya said. "I mean, yes, it's the most exciting thing, but not everyone wants it to happen. Don't you remember that night at dinner last week when Craig and those guys were mad that they couldn't audition?"

"Do you think Craig's responsible?" Analisa asked, with a worried expression.

"Well, no," Maya said. "But someone definitely is."

"So what do we do?" Analisa asked.

"We spy," I said matter-of-factly.

Analisa sat down on the couch and hugged a throw pillow to her chest. "What do you mean?"

"I mean, we take advantage of being right in the middle of it all and pay closer attention to what's going on," I explained.

"But aren't the cops investigating?" Maya asked.

"Yeah, but they aren't as close to the situation as we are," I said. "We're in a much better position to snoop and figure things out. People expect the police to investigate, so they watch their backs when they're around. But nobody would suspect us of trying to solve the case."

"I think you've been reading too many Nancy Drews," Analisa grumbled. "Get real."

"I'm serious," I said. "We could do this."

"I'm in," Maya said. "If it helps get suspicion away from Dani, I'm all for it."

"You guys are crazy," Analisa said.

"No, it'll be fun!" I said. "Just like James Bond. Ooh, could we wear cool Bond Girl costumes? Micro minis, sunglasses, maybe even a wig. I can picture it now — Special Agent Daniela Spevak, Codename: DANCER!"

Maya laughed. "Analisa? You in?"

The sophomore twirled a curl aimlessly around her finger. "I don't know ... "

"Come on, Ana," Maya pleaded. "If someone really is sabotaging the show, then it'll only get more serious. If we don't stop it before it goes any further, they might even cancel the show."

Analisa rolled her eyes. "They're not gonna cancel the show. Kat's in the hospital, and they're not even postponing anything. They'll just find another alternate, like they did with you. And if they do cancel, it won't be the end of the world."

"What?" My voice jumped an octave or two.

"I'm here to study ballet. Not ballroom. Sure, it's fun, but I don't think the New York City Ballet is going to care whether I samba'ed with a musician or not."

"Not all of us studied in Russia last summer. I doubt I have a shot at a company," Maya said. "I need this exposure."

"Maya's right," I said. "We need to figure it all out."

"But wouldn't it be even more dangerous for us to snoop around?" Analisa asked.

"Not if we're careful," I said.

Analisa shook her head. "I'm not sure I really like this idea."

"That's okay. You don't have to," Maya said. "Dani and I'll do it, and you can just stay here and play with your Barbies."

"You're hilarious, you know that?" Analisa rolled her eyes again. "Sorry, but I just don't think it's a good idea. We should let the police do their job. They're trained to investigate. We're not."

"Um, hello? We wouldn't be investigating," I said. "We'd be spying. There's a difference."

"And what are we going to do if we find the saboteur?" Analisa placed her hands on her hips and stuck her chin out defiantly. "Subdue him with a *battement* to the knee caps, and then force him to fall to the floor in a *plié* until the cops arrive?"

"Okay, so it's not completely thought-out yet," I admitted.

Maya picked up a notepad and pen from the coffee table. "We just need a plan."

"Ooh, and we need a Plan B, too," I said, jumping up. "In the movies, they always have a Plan B, and that's the one that always works." I paused for a second, and then did an impromptu *pirouette*. "In fact, scrap that. Maybe we should just start with Plan B. And we need a Plan C, just in case."

"Please don't go all TMZ-trainwreck on me." Analisa collapsed in her chair. If they ever wanted to make one of those comedy-and-tragedy masks for "defeat," they should copy her face at that moment. "*Dios mio*, I'm surrounded by crazies."

By five-thirty we'd formulated a plan. Sorta kinda. Maybe? We'd do double-duty at rehearsal, on the set, and around campus, keeping our ears to the ground for any gossip or clues. We didn't exactly know what we were looking for, but what can you do? Details.

I took a shower and got dressed, not completely sure if I still had a date with Nick Galliano, or whether he'd cancel, thinking I was a wannabe terrorist. Considering my batting average when it came to dates since I'd arrived in Scottsdale (I still couldn't believe Craig stood me up!), I wasn't exactly holding my breath.

Around six-fifteen, my cell phone rang. I nearly tripped over my roommate's art supplies as I ran across the small dorm room and snuck a peak at the Caller ID.

Nick!

"Hello?" I answered, this weird breathy thing going on with my voice.

"Hey Dani, what room you in?" His voice was even sexier over the phone, if that was possible.

"301 Ames Hall." I paused. Now or never. "But are you sure you want to go out with me?"

"Yeah, why?"

"Well ... " I wasn't sure how to answer. "Um, it's just that, um, well Mr. Hawkins thinks I planted the bomb."

He laughed on the other end of the line. "Nobody thinks you did that. Some psycho just put it in your dance bag because it was out in the lobby and was convenient."

"But he was staring right at me. He thinks I did it."

"That's just your imagination."

"I guess so." I paused. Should I tell him? Yeah. Honesty's so important in a relationship. I definitely didn't want to start off on the wrong foot. "My friends and I are going to try to figure out who's behind it all." I heard a sharp intake of breath on the other end of the line, so I knew I'd made a mistake and went back to my awkward ways. "Uh, well, maybe not."

"I hope not. It's a job for the police. So, can you be ready in ten?"

My heart raced. He still wanted to go out with me!

About ten minutes later, my cell rang again. It was Nick, downstairs waiting for me. I shouted a quick bye to Bev, who was way too engrossed in *World of Warcraft* to notice or care, and ran downstairs to meet my date.

My date! I liked the way it sounded.

Nick leaned against the side of the building, looking like an updated Greek god in his distressed dark-wash jeans. He smiled when he saw me, which sent a jolt of energy coursing right through my body, almost like I'd chased a Venti Double Shot Starbucks Mocha with a Red Bull.

Um, not that I've ever done that. On purpose, I mean.

"Hi," I said, taking a step closer, not terribly comfortable walking in my new heels, but Maya made me wear them. She swore up and down they'd make my legs look longer. When you're as short as I was, you took any help you could get. Sometimes you gotta suffer in the name of beauty.

That's when I noticed we weren't alone. JMC sat on the bench in front of the dorm smoking. Yuck. Did he really think that habit was cool?

"Hey, Dani," Nick said, giving me a kiss on each cheek just like they do in France. "You look great. So, my boy JMC's coming with us. We just need to get Hadley and then we can go."

Wait a second ... Stop the presses! My first real date, and I had to spend it with Hadley Taylor? Not exactly the romantic scene I'd been imagining.

Deep breath, Dani. Deep breath.

"Great! It'll be fun to get to know her better," I said, way more enthusiastically than I felt. "So, what dorm is she in?"

"Taylor," JMC answered, snuffing out his cigarette.

Figures she'd live in the dorm named after her dad.

We made awkward small talk as we walked to Hadley's dorm. Again, I was struck by not knowing what to say to Nick, and having JMC there didn't help.

After what felt like a lifetime, Hadley finally deigned to grace us with her presence. She was dressed in what could only be described as Preps Gone Wild: skintight black leather pants with a cropped red plaid tweed jacket over a belted white sweater vest and a crisp button-down. I couldn't imagine why she'd want to wear that heavy jacket in the desert heat. Slung over her arm was a jumbo black patent leather tote. She looked like she'd just stepped off the set of *Pretty Little Liars*. Although the outfit seemed a bit bizarre for the Southwestern surroundings, even I had to admit she looked pretty darn hot.

JMC let out a long, appreciative whistle. "Damn girl," he said, his eyes surveying every inch of her body and then finally coming to rest around chest level. Maybe Maya was right. I'd swear Hadley's boobs were store-bought. They looked about as real as her ID.

Hadley smiled. "Well, it's a special night."

"Hi, Hadley," I said.

"Oh, hello, Danielle."

"Daniela, but everyone calls me Dani."

She waved her perfectly manicured daggers in the air. "Whatever."

"So, where do you suggest we go eat?" Nick asked, not taking his eyes off the blonde teen queen.

Um, hello? I'm here, too. (Why, oh why, weren't my boobs bigger?)

Hadley shrugged, a bored expression on her lovely face as she examined her perfectly manicured nails. "Unfortunately, there's really not much on this side of town. If you like Thai, I guess we could go to Bangkok Bistro."

"Awesome, I love Thai. Dani?" Nick looked my direction.

Just great. There wouldn't be much I could eat in a cuisine

known for slathering everything in peanut sauce. At least I wouldn't have to worry about breaking my diet.

"Um, okay."

"Then Thai it is," JMC said.

And that's pretty much how the rest of the night went. The two guys hung on Hadley's every word, like she was announcing her plan for world peace or giving her Nobel Prize acceptance speech or something. I bet if she let out a fart, they would bottle it up and use it as the base for an expensive perfume. You'd almost think they've never met a beautiful girl before, which was weird, considering JMC had once been linked in the tabloids with both Lohans.

I just wish I'd brought a sweater, because the A/C in the restaurant seemed to be set to sub-zero and I was freezing. No wonder Hadley was dressed like a New England prep.

The sole saving grace was that the restaurant agreed to specially make my Pad Thai without the peanut sauce. At least eating gave me something to do other than watch the guys flirt with Hadley. I mean, hello, was I invisible or something?

Normally when I'm out to dinner with other girls, at least one of them will accompany me to the restroom for a lip-gloss-and-gossip session. Even though Hadley and I didn't like each other much, tonight's dinner was no different. There's nothing like a trip to the bathroom to instill a sense of girl bonding.

Or not.

When we got to the restroom, Hadley dropped a bomb. Okay, in light of the day's events, maybe that wasn't exactly the best choice of words. But she really surprised me with her comments. I mean, I knew we weren't ever going to sit up all night, brush each other's hair, and tell secrets, but I definitely didn't think what happened next was called for.

"Apparently affirmative action is alive and well at the Mountain Shadows Academy," she said, leaning against the sink and staring straight at me, smirking.

"Excuse me?" I asked, not understanding.

"I mean, seriously, Maya Sapp and Analisa San Miguel? Seriously? The producers clearly just wanted to fill their quotas."

Was she implying what I thought she was implying? I could

feel my blood boil. How could she just insult my friends like that? They're two of the best dancers at the school, if not the best. "They were really good in their auditions. You saw them. They belong on the show."

Hadley examined her nails again. Was there anything left to inspect? "Colleen, Arielle, and Rebecca were way better." She looked back up, a scowl marring her face. "They should be in the show, but no, the producers need to get minorities to watch. Typical. And Maya wasn't even supposed to be on the show. How convenient" — she emphasized the word with a sneer and air quotes — "that when the set piece fell, the black girl got to take the white girl's place."

What a bigot! (Yes, I could think of another B word that would work just as well here.) Maya and Analisa definitely both belonged there. I mean, it stunk that Kat had to get hurt for Maya to get in, but I'd watched during rehearsal, and they were absolutely exquisite dancers.

Much better than, well, than ... me.

She must have been able to read my mind or something. "And let's not even start with why the producers chose you." She threw her head back and cackled. Yes, cackled. "I'm sure it was some kind of weird moral lesson or something. You know, 'you don't have to have an awesome body' or some other role model crap like that."

Ouch.

"But I'm sure they're regretting their decision now," Hadley continued, a smug expression on her face.

I clenched my fists and took a deep breath, not wanting to make a scene. I counted to ten before answering. "Well, I'm sorry that you feel that way, Hadley." And then I turned on my heel and marched out of the bathroom.

Kill 'em with kindness. My mom would be so proud.

When we returned to the table, my leftovers were boxed up and waiting for me, just like I'd asked. I looked down and saw that "DANI" was scrawled in the Styrofoam. Nick also had leftovers, with the same messy handwriting.

What a sweetie!

As we got ready to leave, Hadley started in again, not

bothering to beat around the bush. "So Danielle, why'd you plant the bomb?"

"What?" I shrieked.

Nick raised his arms between us as a barrier. "Ladies, ladies. Everyone knows Dani didn't do anything. Calm down. We need to remember why we're here." He glanced down at his soda, and then picked it up as if offering a toast. "To *Teen Celebrity Dance-Off.*"

Hadley narrowed her icy blue eyes. "May the best girl win."

CHAPTER 5

It didn't get any better on the way home. Well, as we started walking back towards campus, Nick put his arm around me, so it started off good, but Hadley wasn't having any of that.

Oh no.

"We can't go home. It's way too early." She pouted in the guys' direction, her voice dripping with Southern Belle sweetness. "There's a really exclusive party ... we should go."

"Sounds good," JMC said.

"Cool," Nick agreed. "Dani?"

I shrugged. "Sure, why not?"

Hadley spun around to face me. "No, Danielle," she said in a really patronizing tone. "I think you misunderstand. We're going to the party, but you're not. It's invitation-only, and sadly, you don't have an invitation." I wanted to wipe the smirk off her face. "I know, because I made up the guest list myself. It's at my parents' house."

So they left ... with very little protest on the guys' part, I might add. I could see JMC going off with her, but Nick? What the heck? Even though I was pissed, I didn't want to be accused of being a diva, so I bit my tongue and had no other choice but to trudge the four blocks back to Ames Hall.

Alone.

"I'm home," I called out. I don't know why I bothered, because Bev had her earbuds in and was ignoring me as usual. Why should tonight be any different? I shoved the leftovers in my mini-fridge, changed into a pair of boxers and a tank top, and went in search of people I could actually talk to.

"What are you guys doing home so early?" I asked, entering the commons room where Maya and Analisa were lounging on the couch watching *Vampire Diaries* reruns. Well, Maya was. Analisa didn't seem to be paying any attention. "I thought you went to dinner with your partners."

"I could ask the same exact question of you," Analisa said, not looking up from painting her nails. Clear polish — how boring. Purple would have been a lot more fun.

"They left to go to some party," Maya explained. "Invitation-only."

I picked up a teal chenille throw pillow and sunk back into the loveseat. "Let me guess — you weren't invited?"

Maya laughed. "How did you know?"

"It's Hadley's party," I said.

Maya shot up off the couch like a deranged jack-in-the-box on caffeine. "This is our big chance! Let's go and investigate."

Analisa capped the nail polish bottle and held her hands up defensively. Or maybe she was just waving her nails dry. I wasn't sure. "Oh no. We're so not going there."

"Come on, don't be such a wimp, San Miguel," Maya teased. "Don't you want to see the legendary Taylor McMansion?"

"We weren't invited, so we'd be crashing, at best, breaking and entering, at worst," Analisa said. "No thanks."

"More than half the cast is there right now," Maya pointed out. "Just think of all the conversations we could eavesdrop on."

"Eavesdropping *is* a big part of spying," I agreed, nudging my toes into the flip-flops under the loveseat.

Analisa pushed a dark curl away from her forehead. "I'm still not convinced we really should be spying."

"Then you stay here," Maya said. "Come on, Dani."

Analisa sighed. "Fine. I'll go. But I really don't think this is a good idea."

We left the dorm and started across the wide green expanse of the quad, totally out of place in the middle of the desert. For about the hundredth time, I was struck by the beauty of the campus. Peach-colored stucco buildings with red-tiled roofs, surrounded by mountains and cacti — if you told me I was on a movie set, I'd believe you. The nearly full moon overhead completed the idyllic scene, as if it was ordered up just for the moment by central casting.

The cool grass tickled my toes as I strode across the lawn. I glanced up and noticed an entire sky full of stars, just like a planetarium or those cheesy glow-in-the-dark stickers that every seven-year-old boy owns. I don't think I've ever seen a night sky that clear. I almost wished I had time to just lie back in the grass and stargaze all night long.

With Nick, of course.

But as we passed Taylor Hall, I was reminded of why he wasn't with me right then. "So, why's Hadley so popular?" I asked. "Because her parents are rich?"

Analisa shrugged. "She's not popular with girls, just the guys."

Maya nodded. "Rumor has it she did it with Craig on their first date."

Analisa turned to Maya with a stern expression. "Maya! Don't gossip. You don't know that's true."

"No, I don't know that for a fact," Maya conceded. "But this is Hadley we're talking about."

Eww. We were on our way to crash one of Hadley's invitation-only parties to which she'd only invited guys. Well, except for her equally obnoxious friends, I mean. Fabulous.

My first attempt at spying wasn't shaping up to be the best idea ever.

"Are you sure we should go?" I asked.

"Why, you wanna turn back?" Analisa asked, a hopeful tinge

creeping into her voice.

"No way," Maya said firmly.

"Uh, guys," Analisa interrupted. "There's no bonfire or anything scheduled for tonight, is there?"

"The first pep rally isn't until mid-September," Maya replied. "Why?"

Analisa gestured off into the distance. "Then we might have a problem, because I see smoke."

Maya and I turned to see what she was pointing at. Sure enough, plumes of smoke and red flames rose from a building on the far side of campus.

"Fire!" I screamed, turning to run.

"The dance studio!" Maya yelled. "We gotta call 911!"

"The studio?" Analisa's voice sounded panicky, matching the pained expression on her face. "So there really was a bomb, after all?"

Maya was already on the phone, reporting the fire. "It looks like Vladirov Studio ... um, I don't know ... yes ... We're on the quad right now ... Okay, we'll do that ... Okay, thanks."

She snapped her cell closed. "The dispatcher wants us to go to our dorm and wait for the police to come take a statement."

"Are they going to put out the fire?" I asked, just as sirens began to wail in the distance for the second time that day.

Maya nodded. "Yeah, they're sending fire engines right now."

By the time we got back to Ames, that morning's bomb scare was old news and all anyone could talk about now was the fire. At least it stopped all the speculation as to whether I'd tried to bomb the studio.

It's the little things that mattered, you know?

But I wasn't so sure that the events weren't linked. It seemed too much of a coincidence that in one day, someone rigged a fake bomb in the same building that was now burning.

And we never did make it down to the party to eavesdrop on the rest of the cast. It was looking more and more like we had a real mystery on our hands, and yet we were totally failing at any attempt to solve it.

Maybe we should stick to dancing. You know, that thing we

all came to Mountain Shadows for in the first place?

I hadn't eaten much at dinner, so I was starving after all the excitement. I made a quick detour back to my room, pulled out my doggie bag, and took it back to Maya's room, where I began to nosh on the leftover Pad Thai. "So, who do you think did it?"

Maya looked up from the book she was reading. "Did what?"

"Set fire to the studio?"

"We don't know anyone did," Analisa said. "The police will be here soon, so we should just let them do their job. It was probably just an accident."

Maya chewed her bottom lip. "I don't think it was an accident. Someone is deliberately sabotaging the show. What do you think Dani?"

By this point, I wasn't really paying any attention to my friends. For some reason, I couldn't breathe. I gasped for breath, but it wasn't working. My air passage was totally constricted. My eyes flooded with tears as I struggled to get air. Not to sound like a drama queen or anything, but I was sure I was going to die.

Analisa ran to my side. "What's wrong?"

"I don't know," I said between sobs. "I—can't—breathe!"

"Is it the smoke?" Maya asked.

I shook my head frantically, unable to speak.

"Are you choking?" Analisa asked.

Maya glanced down at my uneaten food. "What are those leftovers?"

"Thai," I gasped, barely able to croak out the short word.

"Thai? Shit. Do you have an EpiPen? Ana, grab some Benadryl," Maya barked. "We've got to get her to the emergency room."

"What's wrong?" Analisa asked, concern flashing in her dark eyes.

"She must be allergic to peanuts!"

CHAPTER 6

The police took our statements at the emergency room. They wanted to know what we knew about the fire, but since that wasn't much, they left shortly after grilling us. I guess we'd convinced them we were telling the truth, and my near-death experience didn't exactly concern them.

The nurse contacted Bangkok Bistro to find out whether they'd used peanut oil in my food. Both the waitress and manager insisted they'd followed my instructions and left all peanut products out of my Pad Thai. They were used to young customers from the arts school with peanut allergies, so they knew how to tweak the recipes to work around them.

"You're okay," Analisa said when we got back home.

Yeah, 'cuz when your throat swelled up like a balloon and you couldn't breathe, you're really okay. Thank goodness Maya jabbed me with my EpiPen. I'm not sure I would have lived to tell the tale.

Maya propped her chin with her fist. "You know what this

means, right?"

"That Dani ate something she's allergic to?" Analisa answered.

"But they didn't put peanuts in," I whispered.

"Are you sure?" Maya asked. She marched across the room to the table, where my leftovers were still sitting open. She picked up the Styrofoam box and brought it over to us. "See!" she said, pointing at the noodles.

Analisa studied the leftovers. "Crushed peanuts!"

"I specially ordered my food," I said, my throat still a little tingly and raspy from not being able to breathe earlier. "And when they brought it over, it was on a different colored plate, to keep it even more separate."

"I think you were poisoned," Maya said, matter-of-factly.

"Okay, so maybe there were peanuts in the dish, but that doesn't mean she was poisoned," Analisa said. "The restaurant probably just messed up. I mean, yeah, it's a really bad mess-up, but there's always peanuts in Pad Thai. They probably just gave her a regular portion."

"But I was eating at the restaurant with no problems," I said. "I would've noticed crushed peanuts."

Maya shrugged. "Maybe someone put it in there later."

"Wouldn't she have noticed that?" Analisa asked.

"Maybe, maybe not. Did anything suspicious happen at dinner?"

I tried to remember. "I don't think so."

"Did you ever get up to go to the bathroom?" Maya asked.

"Well, yeah."

Maya studied my face, her eyes pleading with me. "So, you don't know what happened at the table when you were in the bathroom, do you?"

"No," I admitted.

"Who was left at the table?"

"I don't remember. Definitely Nick and JMC. Maybe Hadley. I don't really remember."

"You don't remember whether Hadley went to the bathroom with you?" Maya asked.

I scrunched up my nose as I tried to think, but after my ER

experience, my mind was a blank. "She might have. I don't know."

"Well, we'll assume she was still at the table," Maya said. "So that makes her a suspect."

Analisa sighed. "You really think Dani was poisoned?"

Maya placed her pen down and stared at Analisa, an expression of disbelief on her face. "Why do you assume she wasn't? First the set falls, then there's a bomb, then a fire, now this. It's pretty obvious. Face it. Someone's out to get us."

The next morning, I woke up feeling like crap. I didn't really feel sick anymore, but I was incredibly dehydrated, like I'd just done a double triathlon sans Gatorade. I had no idea how I was going to rehearse in this condition. And sad to say, that was probably the point.

Analisa might be a skeptic, but Maya was right. It looked more and more likely that someone was sabotaging the show.

Despite my throbbing head, I grabbed a legal pad, flipped to a new page, and began a list.

> Reasons someone would sabotage the show:
> 1. Jealousy?
> 2.

Hmm ... I couldn't come up with a number two. Minor setback, right? I just needed suspects. I placed my pen against my lips, stared at the ceiling, and let my thoughts drift to when I'd helped Mom organize her notes for trial. She always brainstormed and came up with every possible angle.

Motive, means, and opportunity ...

Okay, I had a motive ... jealousy. That was as good a motive as any. Seven deadly sins and all that. So who was jealous?

Kat, right? She had to be jealous that she got kicked out of the cast after she got hurt. But that didn't make any sense, because, well, she obviously wouldn't have caused her own accident.

So who else?

Craig. That was a given. And Kyle, Tim, and Ryan. Not to mention, Colleen, Arielle, and Rebecca.

Actually, come to think of it, most of the other students at the school were jealous. The so-called "cast of thousands."

I wasn't getting anywhere, was I?

Ding!

Someone was IM'ing me. I glanced at the red digital numbers on my alarm clock. Seven on a Sunday morning. Who in their right mind would be up at this ungodly hour?

I dragged my pathetic butt out of bed, eased my body into the chair in front of the computer, and did a double take.

Mom?

MichelleSpevak:
Hi honey. Dad set this IM account up for me. Are you OK? The hospital called me last night. You're probably sleeping right now, but give me a call when you wake up. I love you!

Well, kind of long for an IM, but at least she was trying.

I typed back:

DaniDancer:
Im awake. Whats up?

Ding!

MichelleSpevak:
LOL! I didn't expect you to be up. I'll call you.

She didn't have all the shorthand down, but apparently someone had taught her what LOL meant. Whitney maybe? Or perhaps one of her assistant DAs.

Seconds later, the phone rang and I flipped it open to answer before it could wake Bev up. The last thing I needed was a pissed-off roommate, although, come to think of it, it's not like she spoke to me anyway.

"Hey Mom."

"Oh honey, how are you feeling? I was so worried when the hospital called last night."

"I'm fine."

"Are you sure? I thought you knew not to eat peanuts."

"I specially order my food, so I don't know what happened."

I could hear the concern in her voice. "Do you need us to come bring you home?"

"No! I'm fine, Mom."

"It's been such a long time since I've spoken to you."

"It's only been four days, Mom."

"Oh, I know, but you're my baby, so I miss you." I cringed as she said "baby." Good thing she couldn't see me. "I heard they're filming a TV show on campus. I bet that's exciting!"

"Actually, I'm on it! I meant to tell you earlier, but I've been so busy."

I was pretty sure she was beaming on the other end of the line. Her voice certainly sounded that way. " Oh Dani! I'm so proud of you."

I smiled. "Thanks. I get to dance with Nick Galliano!"

She laughed. "Um, okay, I'm not sure who that is, but I'm sure it's good."

We continued to chat about the show, and even though it was on the tip of my tongue the whole time, for some reason, I just couldn't tell her about the sabotage. Sure, it would've been great to bounce ideas off her — after all, she's a prosecutor, so she works with the police to solve crimes all the time — but she takes her job as a mom even more seriously than her job as a lawyer. There's no way she'd let me stay at school if she knew about bomb threats and food poisoning. She'd get right onto Expedia, buy a plane ticket, and drag me back, kicking and screaming, to New Jersey.

No thank you. Besides, I'd seen enough *Law and Order* episodes to muddle my way through on my own. How difficult could it be?

After we hung up, I still felt like I needed to talk to someone, so I hit "two" on my speed dial.

"Hello?" My sister's groggy voice came through the phone.

"Hey Whit."

"Dani?"

"Yeah, how are you?"

"What time is it?" She sounded like she had a hangover. Late night? That would make two of us.

"Seven-fifteen here. Ten-fifteen for you."

"Oh my God, Dani, can you just call me later in the day?"

"Um, I guess so." I sighed. "Oh, so did you hear I'm going to be on *Teen Celebrity Dance-Off?*"

"That's awesome!" She seemed to perk up a little. "Who are you dancing with?"

"Nick Galliano."

"Holy shit, Dani! He's totally hot."

"I know."

"Okay, so I'd love to gossip with you more, but I need to get to sleep. Can we talk later?"

I sighed again. Guess it was getting to be a habit. "I guess I'll just go back to my own little life."

Whitney laughed. "Ever the drama queen."

"I'm not a drama queen. I just don't know what to do."

"What's wrong?"

I shrugged, even though she couldn't see me. "IDK, it just seems like someone's out to get us."

Whitney's voice grew serious and she morphed into pre-law mode. "Daniela, what do you mean?"

Suddenly, the stress of audition week and everything got to me and I just couldn't take it anymore. I broke down crying and opened up, words spilling out of my mouth like verbal vomit. "First, a piece of the set fell and this girl ended up in the hospital. But nobody thought anything of it because it seemed like it was just an accident. Then there was a bomb—"

"A bomb?"

"It wasn't a real bomb," I explained between sobs. "But it looked like one, and everyone thinks it was me, but I didn't do anything. I swear!"

"Are you okay?"

"And then the studio started burning down, but I didn't have anything to do with that either. I still don't know if I'm supposed to go to rehearsal today, and on top of all that, my throat swelled up and I couldn't breathe." I hiccupped as I stumbled over my words.

"Did you use your EpiPen?"

"Apparently I ate peanuts, but I didn't mean to. I specially ordered the Pad Thai with no peanuts, but somehow I still got sick."

"Did you use your EpiPen?"

"Yes."

"Dani, Dr. Galloway said that an attack could be fatal!"

"I know." I didn't know what else to say, so I didn't say anything. I know this sounds like a cliché, but the silence was deafening.

"Dani, do you need me to come get you?" my sister finally asked.

Tempting. "I guess so ... "

Wait a second, what was I saying? I didn't need my Big Sister to come rescue me. I was almost fifteen. I could handle this myself.

"I mean, no," I continued, wiping my eyes with my sleeve and trying to regain my composure. "No, I'm fine."

"Were you anywhere near the bomb or the fire?"

"It wasn't a real bomb."

"Are you sure?"

"The bomb squad checked it out."

"Daniela, I'm not sure I like—" Man, she was sounding more and more like Mom.

"Whit ... "

"Are you okay?"

"I'm fine!" I yelled. Bev stirred and glared at me, so I knew I better lower my voice.

"I'm going to tell Mom. She'll know what to do."

"No, Whit, it's okay," I said. "We're gonna solve the case ourselves."

"What case?" she asked. "And who is 'we'?"

"Me, Analisa, and Maya. They're on the show with me."

"Daniela, no. This is a matter for the police."

"But we have it under control." My voice was getting whiny again, but I couldn't help it.

"Bombs and fires aren't exactly what I'd consider under control." She sighed on the other end of the line. "You need to let the police handle this, Daniela. This is not a game."

"We are letting the police handle it. And I can protect myself. Remember those self-defense classes Mom forced me to take? I'm finally doing something that I love for the first time in my life and I don't want you to ruin it!"

"Dani, no offense, but you're an idiot. You can't do this. You're just a little kid."

"I'm fifteen!"

"No, you're fourteen. But that's not the point. You better leave this to the police. They're trained to do this type of thing."

"But we've got it under control."

"Oh really? Then why did you call me?"

"Because you're my sister?" I attempted reason. "I'm supposed to call you."

"Dani ... "

"Whit, I know you and Mom and Dad all think I'm a stupid little kid, but I'm going to do this!" I knew my voice was well into "Dying Swan" territory, but I didn't care. "We can handle it. My friends can figure it out if we put our heads together!"

It felt like five minutes passed before my sister spoke again, although it was probably under ten seconds. "Okay, fine. I won't mention it to Mom and Dad. But you have to promise me you'll call the police if anything else happens." She paused. "And me, too."

"We won't do anything to put ourselves in danger," I said. "I just want to dance."

CHAPTER 7

The rest of the day went much more smoothly. The damage to the
dance building wasn't extensive enough to cancel any rehearsals.
Fortunately, the fire was confined to Studio B, and hadn't spread
to any of the other studios, so there was still sufficient practice
space. All it meant was that Nick and I had to move to Studio G
to learn our second dance, jive. G was larger and brighter
anyway. No biggie.

The McCauleys worked with us for a couple of hours until it
was time for the camera crew to come in and film some candid
footage of the two of us practicing our routine. Candid? Snort.
We redid those takes about fifty times.

"Shouldn't they just continuously shoot the session?" I
whispered. "Then they'd get a lot of footage, and they could edit
in and out whatever they wanted."

Nick laughed. "Dani, they have to make sure it's right."

"But isn't this a reality show?"

"Yeah, but they want to set up the screw-ups so they have a

good contrast for when we perform live," Nick explained.
I frowned. "How is that reality?"
"It's TV."
"Let's do the fall again," the cameraman commanded.

Nick and I walked to the center of the room for him to once again drop me on my butt, so the producers could get maximum laugh-factor out of the segment. I was disillusioned by how unrealistic reality TV really was, not to mention my body ached all over.

Finally, after Nick dropped me another ten times and the camera crew had filmed us from every possible angle and even a few impossible ones, the director asked us to do it "once more from the top." Fortunately, this time we were allowed to do it right.

The opening strains of "Jailhouse Rock" filled the studio. Nick shook in time to the beat like Elvis. He made eye contact and beckoned me over, just as the McCauleys had choreographed, only this time it didn't feel like we were just going through the motions. I strolled across the floor and he caught my arm and spun me towards him, culminating in a low dip before we busted out the dance steps.

Step-ball-change, step-ball-change, rock-step
Step ball change, step ball change, rock step
Step-ball-dig-spin, step-ball-dig-spin
Step-ball-change, step-ball-change, rock-step

I even forgot about the cameras. All I concentrated on was Nick and the magic we were creating. If the sparks were any indication, then all he was concentrating on was me. The atmosphere in the studio was so electric, so intense, so amazing that I knew we'd have a great chance of winning the competition if we performed just like that on stage.

Swivel-kick
Swivel-kick
Swivel-kick
Shimmy-shimmy

As Nick spun me around and around, the entire camera crew fell away. Finally, as the music came to a close, he whipped me towards him and lifted me off the ground, ending in a sort of lunging dip.

We held that final pose for a second or two after the music ended. I looked into his eyes, like steaming mugs of hot chocolate, and was once again struck by the magical sensation that he was going to kiss me.

But just as before, he didn't.

No, there was no bomb scare this time. Instead, the camera crew began clapping and cheering. Nick dropped my gaze, turned to face his admiring crowd, and took a bow. Had it been the final scene of a romantic comedy, we would've ended in a passionate kiss, but well, I guess I had to remember although he was an actor, I was no leading lady.

I followed his lead and curtseyed. That's when I noticed that somehow, in the middle of our routine, Mr. Hawkins and his black-clad assistant, Tracy, had slipped into the studio unnoticed. I expected him to scowl and accuse me of plotting to bomb the studio, but instead he smiled and applauded.

Would wonders never cease?

"Bravo! Wonderful job!" Mr. Hawkins strode towards us. "I need you over in the theatre for a cast meeting."

Ten minutes later, we all sat in a circle onstage in the main theatre, just like that first night when the set piece fell. It had been less than forty-eight hours and yet it felt like a lifetime. So much had changed.

Mr. Hawkins strode to the center of the circle, Tracy following him. "Ladies and gentlemen, I wanted to get you all together to congratulate you on a wonderful first two days of rehearsing. From what your choreographers have indicated, you have each done remarkably well on your first two dances, particularly in light of the most unfortunate circumstances. We have gotten some simply extraordinary footage."

Tracy stood behind him, still clutching that same clipboard. Did she ever put it down? "Now it's time to switch gears and learn a different style. In ballroom, there are two different syllabi,

American and International. You're each learning the International syllabus," she said. "In the International syllabus, there are two styles: Latin and Standard."

"Yesterday, you each learned two of the Latin dances: cha-cha, rumba, samba, paso doble or jive. When danced in that order, they tell a story, but that is only when you do each one. Not yet. You are not yet at that point, but you will be soon. Please keep practicing," Mr. Hawkins said. "Next Saturday, you'll be learning one of the Standard dances: waltz, Viennese waltz, tango, foxtrot, or quickstep."

Tracy handed out slips of paper to each couple. "This is the next dance you'll each be learning."

I glanced at the piece of paper in Nick's hands. Foxtrot? I knew nothing about the foxtrot, except that Fred Astaire and our school's founder, Anna Devereaux, did it in all those old movies.

I peeked over my shoulder at Analisa's slip of paper. Tango. How did she get such a cool dance?

"Nick and Daniela, you're dancing the cha-cha, jive, and the foxtrot," Tracy said, looking at her clipboard. "Daronn and Analisa, you will be doing the jive, paso doble, and the tango. John Michael and Hadley, the samba, rumba, and Viennese waltz. Carson and Maya, the cha-cha, rumba, and the quickstep."

"You will continue to rehearse your Latin dances, and then next Saturday you will learn your Standard dance. Please pay careful attention. You'll get exactly one week and one day to rehearse the Standard dance, and then we go live on national television in front of potentially millions of viewers exactly two weeks from today." Mr. Hawkins peered at us over his glasses. "Do not embarrass me."

Hadley raised her hand, a bored expression on her face. "Are we still going to go on?"

"Of course, Miss Taylor," Mr. Hawkins said. "I just explained that we will be going live two weeks from today."

"But in light of recent events—"

"We have invested a great deal of money producing this show."

Hadley scowled. "Are you sure it's safe? My father says—"

Mr. Hawkins waved his hand in dismissal. "Miss Taylor, I

understand that your father is a big donor to this school; however, he is not funding this television show. I make the decisions around here. We will go forward as planned."

I wish you could have seen it. Hadley's face in response was just classic.

"We've arranged for a private security firm to provide some extra security around the set," Tracy said, clutching her clipboard to her chest.

"But what about while we're in class?" Maya asked.

"It is our belief that any potential setbacks are confined to the show alone," Mr. Hawkins explained.

"Setbacks?" Maya whispered to me. "Please tell me he didn't just actually call two girls going to the hospital a 'setback.'"

"Don't forget the bomb and the fire," I whispered back.

"But because we cannot afford to have anything stop the show from going on, we have arranged for Detective Dan Carroll of Metro PD to speak with you tonight to assuage any uneasiness," Mr. Hawkins continued.

A tall plainclothes officer with dark blond, close-cropped hair walked into the center of the circle, towering over us as we sat. He stood ramrod straight, like a Marine in an inspection line. He studied the cast carefully and then cleared his throat before beginning.

"We have been looking into the events of the past couple of days. Unfortunately, it appears that this cast and this show are the victims of sabotage." His eyes swept over the now-murmuring crowd. "We're taking measures to protect you all from any future danger. It is our belief that these are childish pranks designed to force a shutdown of filming and are not truly dangerous. However, we'll be placing full-time security on the campus. I assure you, this investigation is a priority for our department."

Hadley raised her hand. "Detective, does the department have any leads?" She looked pointedly in my direction.

Detective Carroll shook his head. "I'm sorry, but I am not able to discuss leads in an active investigation. Although it's our belief that this is just a series of pranks, arson is a serious crime."

"So it definitely was arson?" Carson asked.

"I'm not at liberty to answer that."

"Did you know that Dani had a food allergy attack last night?" Maya asked.

"I hardly think that has to do with this case," Tracy interrupted.

"Actually," Detective Carroll interrupted. "The hospital contacted us this afternoon. The toxicology report from the takeout box you provided has come in, and it appears that Ms. Spevak did in fact ingest some peanuts or peanut oil last night."

"But that's impossible. I watched her special order her food," JMC said.

"Yes, and the staff at Bangkok Bistro claims that they prepared it to her specifications." Detective Carroll shrugged. "My guess is that they meant to, but there was probably a trace of peanut oil on the pan." He turned to face me. "If I were you, young lady, I'd stop eating at Bangkok Bistro. But I assure you all, it has nothing to do with this case."

CHAPTER 8

On Monday morning, my academic classes seemed to drag on For. Ev. Er. I always wished they'd just hurry up so I could get to dance class anyway, but it didn't exactly help today that all the other kids whispered instead of conjugating their French irregular verbs and pointed at me while they dissected the poor little innocent frogs. And, really, could you blame them? I mean, it's not every day that you have a real live shoe-bomber in your class.

I cursed my mom for making me start taking French lessons in seventh grade. If I'd waited until high school, I would have been in a beginner class with the other freshmen, but no, I had to be in French III with sophomores and juniors.

And that meant Hadley. Damn.

My sole saving grace was that Maya and Analisa were in there, too. Of course, so were lots of other kids, and they wouldn't shut up.

I got so sick and tired of having to constantly explain that I had nothing to do with the sabotage and the police didn't have any suspects yet, I eventually gave up entirely. Taking a page from my mom's playbook, I started answering "no comment."

"How do you say that in French?" Maya whispered to me.

"What?" I asked.

She laughed. "'No comment.' What would that be? *'Pas de comment?'"*

"That's not what *comment* means in French," Analisa whispered, pronouncing the word 'co-mon.' "It means 'how.'"

"*Mesdesmoiselles!*" Madame Renaud's shrill voice jerked us out of our little *sotto voce tête à tête.* (Some people mixed metaphors; I preferred to mix languages.) She crossed her arms and lifted her chin. *"Ici, nous parlons français."*

"*Comment dites en français,* 'bomb'?" Hadley asked, looking right at me.

Just great. She was asking how to say "bomb" in French.

"*Comment dites en français,* 'bitch'?" Maya muttered. Yeah, she had my back.

"*Mademoiselle* Sapp!" Madame's eyes bored right into Maya.

"*Desolée,*" Maya mumbled, even though she didn't really look all that sorry.

Once Madame turned to face the other side of the class, Analisa nudged Maya and said, with a wink, "I believe the word you're looking for is *'chienne.'"*

Yeah, they're sparkotastical. (What? I liked sparkly things, and I liked making up words. Shakespeare did it all the time, so why couldn't I?)

After struggling through French, English, Biology, and Geometry, it was finally time for my second dance class of the day. On Mondays, right before lunch, I had a forty-minute barre workout, followed by twenty minutes of variations. On Tuesdays, I did yoga. Wednesday was tap. Thursday, contemporary. And Friday, another ballet class.

In the two weeks since school started, I'd come to decide that this late morning time slot was my favorite part of the day. An opportunity to relax and forget about all my stress and just throw myself into my art. But today, well, let's just say things weren't exactly going that well.

I took my usual place at the front of the barre, and had just sunk into my first *plié* when whispers rolled across the room like the start of an April rain— just a trickle at first and then it all came crashing at me. The live music from the accompanist didn't come close to drowning out the nagging questions and rumors.

"So, Dani," the girl behind me whispered. "Why'd you do it?"

"No comment," I said for about the hundredth time, through gritted teeth as I tried to follow the barre exercise.

"Isn't that what they always say when they're guilty?" the short boy on the center barre asked.

"Shh!" our instructor Grigor Dmilov snapped. "Ladies and gentlemen, we are doing *pliés*, not gossip. Talk all you want later. But now we dance."

I tried to drown out my classmates by concentrating on the exercise. Why, oh why, wasn't Maya in this class? I'm sure she could've run interference with the firing squad. She's my girl, you know? But no. Just my luck, she had to be in contemporary class this morning.

"They shouldn't have picked her," the girl behind me continued. "I bet the producers are regretting it now."

"Do you think she faked the allergy attack?" another girl asked.

"No, she snuck some peanut oil in there so she could get sick and then blame it on someone else," the first girl said. "That's what Hadley said."

"I'm warning you," Monsieur Dmilov said. "And one-two-three-four ... "

I closed my eyes as I continued the exercise, taking a deep breath and counting to ten before opening them again. I tried to picture myself in a Zen-like state. I knew I couldn't say anything to them, but it was taking all my restraint to keep from doing so.

As I stretched my upper body towards the barre, it hit me that perhaps this was just jealousy, pure and simple. I'd probably hate the girls on the show, too, if I weren't on it.

Finally we moved to the center of the room, where Monsieur Dmilov taught us a *petit allegro* combination. All those jumps made me short of breath, but there was no way I would admit it and give those bitches a reason to doubt I deserved to be on the show. After about twenty minutes of the demanding physical torture of *brisées*, *assemblées*, and *changements*, we were finally excused. I knew Maya would probably expect me to stick around and snoop, but I was in no mood to face my tormentors. Instead, I rushed off to the dining hall.

Craig and his cronies, Tim, Kyle, and Ryan, were across the room, surrounded by a big group of girls and boys. For once Craig wasn't the center of attention. Kyle was holding court, gesturing at what appeared to be a new flyer. But I didn't have time to worry about it. I needed to grab a salad and get back to the dorm.

I rushed through the line, picking up small pre-packaged tossed salad with a peach lowfat yogurt and a large bottle of water. As I was handing my student ID to the cashier so she could swipe it through the card reader, I overheard a conversation behind me.

"Are you signing the petition?"

"Yeah, I think so. It's complete crap we couldn't try out."

"What about all the crazy stuff that's happening? Won't that shut it down?"

"Oh, you mean the bomb? I heard some freshman chick did that."

"Yeah, Danielle Spevak."

Daniela Spevak, you idiot. Or Dani. At least get my name right if you're gonna talk shit about me.

"Yeah, what a head case. I heard she rigged the set to fall on Kat Holmes. Crazy. Who'd want to hurt Kat? She's the nicest girl here."

"I hope they kick her off the show."

"Then they'd need to replace at least one slot."

"Yeah. Wouldn't that be great?"

Part of me wanted to spin around and give those gossips a piece of my mind (okay, really just a good slap in the face), but my more rational self took control and convinced me that I shouldn't get into any trouble, now of all times. Sure, catfights make for great ratings on reality shows, but the producers had

59

made it clear that they couldn't afford any scandals.

Suddenly I wasn't so hungry after all.

I grabbed my ID back from the cashier and left the salad right there as I marched over to Craig and his friends.

"Oh hello, Dani." He flashed me a killer smile.

Normally I would have blushed when he did that, but spending time with Nick Galliano had shown me that Craig wasn't exactly all that. Besides, I was pissed about what everyone had been saying about me.

"Hi Craig. What's going on over here?" I asked, my hands planted firmly on my hips.

"Feeling better today?" he asked.

"Yes, thank you. Care to answer my question?"

"I'm sorry about the other day. I can expl—"

"My question, please."

He fixed an intense gaze on me that was probably designed to make me swoon, but really just made me madder. "Uh, Kyle can help you then."

Kyle smirked. "Do you want to join our cause?"

"And what cause would that be?"

Tim passed me a flyer. "You're probably not interested, since you're already on the show, but we're trying to drum up support for the ACLU to take our case."

I grabbed the flyer from him.

Stand up for an America that's color blind and gender blind.
Boycott Teen Celebrity Dance-Off's discriminatory audition policies!

He had to be freaking kidding me.

"Discriminatory audition policies?" I asked.

"That's right, Dani. Discriminatory audition policies." Kyle leaned back against the lunch table like Big Man on Campus. Probably been studying his arrogant friend's behavior. I secretly wished he'd fall over. That would be pretty funny. "Only girls were allowed to try out. The school's discriminating against males. And not just males, but white males in particular. That seems to be the popular group to discriminate against these days and nobody seems to ever care."

"Oh, please," I said, dropping the flyer on the table, my fists clenching. "There are plenty of white males on the show: Nick Galliano, JMC, not to mention the producer, Mr. Hawkins."

"Yeah, but what about students?" Ryan piped up. "No male students of any race are on the show. Just girls."

"It's discrimination, pure and simple. And it's illegal." Craig's blue eyes pierced right through me. "We're gonna win this one, so you might as well sign."

I rolled my eyes. "Whatev," I said, turning to leave.

"Where are you going?" Kyle asked.

"To my room. Do I need your permission?"

"Well, be careful. I wouldn't want you to run into any bombs or fires," Kyle responded with a smirk.

CHAPTER 9

"Guess who I ran into in the caf," I announced as I walked into the commons room.

"Let me guess." Maya looked up from her copy of Melissa Francis' *Love Sucks* and rolled her eyes. "You were accosted by a group of obnoxious drama students demanding that you sign their stupid petition for a ridiculous lawsuit that isn't going anywhere."

I sat down on the floor and began some stretches. "You too?"

"Why do you think we're in here?" Analisa asked, spearing a piece of lettuce for emphasis. "Where's your lunch?"

"I'm not hungry," I said, as I leaned over my left leg.

Maya eyed me carefully. "Seriously, Dani, you eat like Nicole Ritchie. What's up with that?"

"Oh, please," I protested. "I eat."

"Barely."

"Well, you wouldn't want to eat, either, if you got food poisoning a couple of days ago," I snapped.

Analisa pursed her lips, like she was weighing her words. "It was before that."

"What are you talking about?"

"You barely ate before the food poisoning, too."

"I eat!"

I guess my friends didn't know what to say, because it got really quiet after that, and I felt like I was back in my own room with the oh-so-talkative Bev. I had to do something.

"Kyle said something really strange," I began.

"*Kyle's* really strange," Maya said, crumbling her sandwich wrapper in a ball, and joining me on the floor in a stretch.

"No, when I was leaving he said something like, 'be careful or you might wind up burned in a fire,'" I said.

Maya's brown eyes lit up. "That sounds like a threat if I've ever heard one. You think he's behind the sabotage?"

I rolled my shoulders to get out all the kinks. "I don't know, but it's a start."

Analisa laughed. "Please, he's harmless."

"Yeah, but Craig's arrogant enough to do just about anything if he thought it might help him get ahead," Maya said.

"But Kyle?" Analisa shook her head. "He's a teddy bear."

"He's a total caboose," Maya said.

"A caboose?"

"A follower. He blindly does whatever his idol Craig tells him to do," Maya explained. "If Craig asked Kyle to jump off the roof of the library, he would. He wouldn't even hesitate. I wouldn't put it past Craig to mention to Kyle that it would make his life much easier if the show couldn't go on."

I scrunched up my nose as I thought about that. "But that doesn't make any sense. I thought Craig wanted to get on the show. How would it help his cause if the show was totally shut down?"

"Yeah. Besides, his girlfriend's on the show," Analisa said, a deep crease forming in her forehead. "He wouldn't do that to Hadley. It's her big break."

"I think you underestimate the true arrogance and Machiavellian nature of Craig Washosky," Maya said. "If I had to make a bet right now, I'd wager any amount he's our guy."

I jumped up and grabbed my book bag. "Keep talking. I'm getting some paper so we can make notes."

"So what do we know?" Maya said. "The first thing that happened was the set fell. Who was around then?"

"We all were. Everyone in the cast," I said. "Mr. Hawkins, Tracy, and that Steve guy."

"Scene one: set falls and hurts Kat. Cast, Mr. Hawkins, Tracy, and Steve present," Analisa said.

"Should I write down our names?" I asked.

Maya nodded. "Yeah, write down everyone."

"What about the other stagehands?" Analisa asked.

"I thought you weren't going to help?" Maya asked, smirking.

"I'm not," Analisa snapped. "But if you're going to insist upon it, I guess I'll just have to go along with your stupid plan. If you can't beat 'em, join 'em."

"Um, I don't know. What other stagehands are there?" I asked.

"Tim sometimes works as a stagehand," Maya said.

"Really?" I put my pen down and sat up straight. "I thought he was an art major?"

"He is, but his buddies Craig and Kyle are actors, so sometimes he lends his flair for design to the theatre," Maya explained.

"So, he could've had access to that flat," I said. "This is all beginning to come together."

I scribbled in the notebook.

> 1. Set piece falls — Friday nite
>   Kat — hurt
>   Dani - no
>   Ana — no
>   Hadley? maybe
>   Daronn? (doubtful)
>   Nick? (doubtful)
>   Carson? (doubtful)
>   JMC? (doubtful)

Mr. Hawkins — no
Tracy — no
Steve? maybe
Other stagehands? Tim might have
had access.

"How can we find out whether Tim was there or not?" I asked.

"We could ask the other stagehands," Maya said.

"But we don't even know who else was working that day," I said. "Just Steve. Maybe there were others, but he was the only one Mr. Hawkins spoke to."

"So we'll start with Steve," Maya said.

"I don't buy it," Analisa said, shaking her head.

"What don't you buy?" Maya asked.

"That Tim had anything to do with this."

I looked up from my notebook. "Well, we know he does set design and he's Craig's friend."

"But it's completely out of character." Analisa frowned. "He's a sweetheart."

"You've gotta watch those quiet ones," Maya said. "Whenever a serial killer gets caught they interview his next-door neighbors who always tell the reporters, 'but he was so quiet, so nice.'"

"Well, whatever. Let's move on to the next event," Analisa said. "The bomb threat."

"It was more than a threat," I said. "Someone actually rigged a fake bomb."

"True," Maya said. "Again, the whole cast was there, and Mr. Hawkins and Tracy. Anyone else?"

"Really anyone could've been there." I chewed on my pen before continuing. "We were all in different studios, and who knows who could've been lurking around in the lobby."

"Okay," Analisa said. "They found it in the lobby. In your dance bag, Dani."

"Thank you," I said, heat flushing my cheeks. "Like I really needed to be reminded."

"I'm not blaming you." Analisa threw away the remains of

her lunch and joined me on the couch. "I'm just wondering, who had access to your bag?"

I thought back. "Um, I don't know. I took it out into the hall so I'd have money to buy myself a snack, but Nick treated me, so I didn't need it and then I forgot to bring it back into the studio."

I scribbled:

> 2. Fake bomb in Vladirov Studio — Sat aft
>   Bomb found in lobby — Who had access?
>   Dani left bag in hall by mistake
> 3. Fire in Vladirov Studio — Sat nite (9-ish)
>   Nick, JMC, Hadley at party; where was Craig?
> 4. Dani ingests peanut oil — Sat nite (7-8:30?)
>   Nick, JMC, Hadley at restaurant

"But Detective Carroll said that was the restaurant's fault," Analisa said, looking over my shoulder as I wrote.

"Until we know for sure one way or the other, let's just assume it has to do with the case," Maya said.

"I'm pretty sure the peanut allergy has nothing to do with the rest of the sabotage," Analisa said. "I mean, Dani was at dinner, and then her dining companions went off to Hadley's party, so they couldn't have set the fire."

"Do we know for sure they went to Hadley's party, or are we just assuming?" Maya asked.

"We're just assuming, but we can easily find that out," I said. "But that would mean you suspect Nick or JMC and that's just ridiculous."

"I didn't say I suspected Nick or JMC," Maya said.

"Then who do you mean?" I asked.

"Who's been nothing but jealous throughout this whole thing?" Maya asked.

I picked up a pillow and punched into it. "Craig?"

"Besides him," Maya said.

"Pretty much everyone on campus," Analisa said. "That doesn't exactly eliminate anyone."

"Okay, not jealous, snotty. And catty. And she was at dinner with you," Maya said.

"Hadley?" I asked.

"Bingo."

"No way," Analisa said with an emphatic shake of her curls. "The show is really good for her career. Why would she jeopardize that?"

"You're right, I don't think she's trying to jeopardize it," Maya said. "But I wouldn't put it past her to try to get rid of some of the competition."

"What do you mean?" I asked.

"Well, some of this stuff that's been happening seems to be focusing blame on you, Dani," Maya explained. "And Hadley's little fembots have been spreading rumors around campus that you're to blame for everything."

"And if I was found responsible, then the producers would have to kick me out of the competition," I said. "You know, I think you might have something there, Maya."

"Hadley did look green with envy when she saw your audition," Analisa agreed.

"But wait. That doesn't even make sense. Why would she be jealous of me?"

"Come on, Dani," Maya said. "Don't be modest. You know you're the best dancer here."

Surely she had to be joking.

"Yeah right," I said defensively. "There are tons of people better than me, and two of them are right here in this suite."

"Oh please, girl," Maya said. "I saw your audition. That Afro-Cuban thing?" She whistled. "Damn, that was hot. You're an awesome dancer."

I looked over at Analisa, but she just nodded.

"Besides," Maya continued, "I didn't even make it into the cast at first. I was just the understudy." She laughed. "If I didn't know any better, I'd say I had a motive to make the set fall."

CHAPTER 10

Around three o'clock I rushed off for a rehearsal with Nick. The girls and I promised that we'd keep our eyes open and ears perked for any possible clues. But we'd made the same promise before, and that hadn't exactly gotten us anywhere.

"Hey Dani." Nick smiled at me as I entered the studio. "Ready to jive?"

"Why couldn't we have gotten a cool dance like the samba?" I grumbled, putting my dance bag down. I spotted my reflection in the floor-to-ceiling mirror and saw that I was scowling. Yikes. That sure wasn't going to win me any votes with Nick.

"You're kidding me, right?" he asked, laughing. "JMC told me that dance is killing him. It's really hard. And anyway, we're already doing a cha-cha for our first dance."

"But the samba is so sexy and fun. We'd totally win over the public." I bent down and touched my toes to stretch out my back. Then I walked my hands forward along the hardwood floor. "We

68

need lots of call-in votes if we're gonna win."

Nick laughed. "I wouldn't worry too much about that, Dani."

"Why not?"

"We'll do just fine with the public."

"No offense, Nick, but you don't exactly have the same draw as JMC or Daronn."

He leaned over and massaged my shoulders, once again sending shivers of electric pleasure coursing all the way down to the tips of my toes. Even hanging upside down, I could feel my heart do a flip-flop. "Relax. We've got it in the bag."

If he kept doing stuff like that, we'd never get any rehearsing done.

"All right, let's get this show on the road." I straightened up and strode over to the stereo system. I needed to put some distance between us so he wouldn't be able to see the bright red glow that I knew was rapidly spreading like a rash across my face. I hit play on the CD player and spun around to face him. "Wanna take it from the top?"

"Aye, aye, m'lady," he said with a fake Cockney accent and an exaggerated bow.

Man, was he cute!

Nick walked to the center of the floor and got into position. As the opening strains filled the small room, he was magically transformed from a 2000s rising star into a 1950s teen idol.

... went to a party in the county jail ...

He shook his hips and flashed me a smile, beckoning me to join him. Like the McCauleys had choreographed, I pretended to hesitate, shaking my head in a coquettish "no." He continued to tease and tempt me, until I finally "gave up" and joined him at center stage for our dance.

We step-ball-changed and shimmied our way around the room, kicking and twirling and laughing the whole time. I'd always loved dancing, but I'd never had so much fun as I did when I was with him. He spun me around and around so fast that I almost didn't notice the face at the window.

"Stop!" I yelled, and shrugged out of his hold.

Nick's brows knit with worry. "What's wrong?"

"There's someone out there!" I said, as I ran to the window and looked out.

"Well, yeah," he said, as he turned off the music. "There's a whole big campus outside. People are always out there."

"No really," I said, squinting to get a better view. "There was a face at the window. Just before, while we were dancing."

"I'm sure it was nothing," he said in a bored voice.

I spun around to face him, my back resting against the barre. "It could be the person who left the bomb! Maybe even set the studio on fire! We need to go after him."

"Was it a man or a woman?"

"IDK," I admitted, feeling my shoulders slump a little. "But whoever it is, he's getting away."

"Dani, let's just get back to practice."

I dug the toe of my ballroom shoe into the rosin box. "No, I'm serious. I saw someone!"

Nick sighed. "Fine. I'll go. But you stay here. If it really is the arsonist, he's dangerous."

He left the room and I was left alone. It would've been the perfect time to snoop, but where would I start?

I heard the music coming from the other studios, all mixed together in a jumble of cacophony so that I couldn't really make out any individual tune. I decided to check out the other rehearsals.

I picked up my bag and stepped out into the hallway. The music abruptly stopped in the studio next door. Maybe I'd check in there, and see how they were doing.

I was about to knock on the door when I heard a beep coming from my cell phone. I dug it out and checked the display.

BUTT OUT OR ELSE

I burst out laughing at the absurdity of the situation and sank into one of the couches. Tears nearly trickled out of my eyes, I was laughing so hard.

I knew it wasn't funny, but for some reason I just couldn't help it. Once I got started, I couldn't stop.

Some people got demand letters. Others got threatening phone calls. Still others got notes with words cut out from magazines. I, on the other hand, got a threat text.

Welcome to the 21st century.

"We'll just go to Detective Carroll. I'm sure he can run a trace and find out who sent you the text," Analisa said.

I shook my head. "I wish it was that simple. I remember from helping my mom on a case. We'll need to get a subpoena."

"You mean like a warrant?" Analisa asked.

"Sort of. Basically, we need a court order." I rested my chin on my hands. "And that's not all that easily obtained. Especially if we want to keep our cover."

Maya nodded. "We definitely don't want to blow our cover. The element of surprise is what's most useful. If people know we're spying on them they won't be willing to open up to us."

"Oh, please," Analisa said, rolling her eyes. "Like they're really opening up to us now. Anyway, somebody already knows. Didn't you see the text message?"

"No, Ana, I didn't get that memo," Maya said, her voice dripping with sarcasm.

"Who do you think knows?" I asked.

Maya shrugged. "You guys been asking questions?"

"Well, yeah," I admitted. "I have, but casually. Kinda. At least I thought it was casual."

Analisa just nodded.

Maya smirked. "That makes all of us. I guess maybe we weren't as subtle as we thought."

"Then why was Dani the only one who got that message?" Analisa asked.

Without saying another word, my friends exchanged glances and then quickly rooted in their bags for their cell phones. No unread text messages.

"Looks like whoever's trying to scare Dani off the case doesn't know about the rest of us," Analisa said.

Maya's face lit up and she slammed her fist on the coffee table, making the rest of us jump. "Or maybe Dani's a clue."

"Me?"

"Well, so far, you've been involved in each of the things that happened," Maya explained.

"You too? We've already been through—"

Maya put up her hand to cut me off. "I know you didn't do any of them. But you were around when all of them happened."

"What does that have to do with anything?" I asked. "We all were."

"Just hear me out." Maya picked up her bottle of Diet Coke and took a large gulp before continuing. "The set fell. Dani was there. The bomb was found in Dani's bag—"

"It wasn't a real bomb."

"—and Dani was with us when we reported the fire. Dani ingested peanut oil. And Dani saw a face at the window." She paused. "Someone's out to get Dani, or Dani's the clue. Either way, Dani has something to do with this."

"I didn't do—"

"I didn't say you were the culprit. I just said that someone seems intent on either setting you up, or getting you off the show, or getting you off the case."

"You know, Maya, I think you might be right." Analisa pushed a dark curl off her face. "We need to look at who Dani's been hanging around lately. Does she have any enemies? Who knows she's snooping?"

"Spying," I corrected.

Analisa practically spoke with her hands. "Snooping, spying, whatever. Who heard her asking questions?"

"Who knows she's allergic to peanuts?" Maya asked.

"You guys know. And so do Nick, JMC, and Hadley," I said. "They all heard me special order dinner at Bangkok Bistro."

"Did anyone else know?" Maya asked.

"I don't think so."

"You know," Analisa said. "I don't think the Pad Thai has

anything to do with the sabotage of the show. And nobody knew ahead of time."

Maya nodded. "You could be right. But it just seems like too much of a coincidence. All this other crazy stuff has been happening. The timing is just weird."

Analisa giggled. "Now I'm convinced you've been watching too much *Veronica Mars*. Didn't you know there's always a red herring? We're concentrating on the peanuts_but totally missing the smoking gun."

I drew a thick red line through the Pad Thai entry in the legal pad timeline. "Yeah, it's like when you really, really want a Dooney or Coach bag and it's all you can think about, so you forget that they actually have really cute bags at Target, and you could probably afford to get a new purse to match every outfit, if you just went there instead."

Maya laughed. "What?"

I sighed with exasperation. "Let's focus on the important stuff. Like the bomb, okay?"

I stretched my legs into a wide second position split on the floor, forming an almost perfectly straight line with my legs, extending from my left toe to my right toe. Boys are always impressed with my flexibility.

But flexibility wasn't exactly going to help me here.

Right then, my phone rang. I glanced at the Caller ID and saw it was Nick.

"I gotta take this," I said to the other girls.

I turned away, not waiting for an answer, and flipped open the cell. "Hello?"

"Hey, babe." I felt myself flush when he said that. How did he always know exactly what to say? "You rushed off so quickly, I didn't get a chance to see you when I got back inside."

"Yeah, sorry. I got a te—" Maya was waving her hands so crazily and jumping up and down so frantically that I nearly dropped the phone. "What's wrong?" I whispered to her.

"What did you say?" Nick asked.

"Uh, nothing," I said. "Can you hold on a sec?"

I fumbled the phone for a second before finding and pressing the mute button, then glared pointedly at Maya.

"Don't tell him about the text," she said.

"Why not?"

"You never show your hand. Keep it on the down low. Need-to-know basis. And he doesn't need to know."

Mixed metaphors, much?

I rolled my eyes. "Fine." I returned to my conversation. "Hey."

I noticed my friends giggling and rolling their eyes. I guess I did go all "fan-girl" when I talked to him, but I really couldn't help it. He was just so, well, perfect.

I had no idea why Hollywood hadn't cast him as a lead in anything. Tons of small parts, but no leads. Big mistake. He had leading man written all over him. Tall, broad shoulders, six-pack, and a profile like he'd just walked right off the picture on a Grecian urn. At seventeen!

"Hey," he said in a low sexy growl, making me all tingly again. "So, are you okay?"

"Yeah, why wouldn't I be?"

"I don't know. But you disappeared before I got back to the studio."

I gave a sort of mirthful smile, even though I knew he couldn't see me. "Sorry. I realized I had to get back here."

"What for?"

Shit. I didn't expect that question. "Um, homework?"

"No prob." There was a pause on the other end of the line. "So, anyway, I didn't find anyone."

"They probably left before you got outside."

He laughed. "Dani, I don't think you saw anyone."

Hmm ... I knew what I saw. "Maybe not. I've always had a really overactive imagination. Maybe I should think about taking some creative writing classes." I paused to think of what I should say next. "I guess I'm just getting a little nervous with all this crazy stuff going on. Do you think someone's trying to sabotage the show?"

"Nah," he said, chuckling. "It's just a bunch of weird coincidences."

We chatted a little longer, but I could tell the conversation was going nowhere. Finally his voice trailed off and then he said an abrupt, "See you around."

I pressed the END key on my phone, a little dejected that he hadn't asked me out for dinner. But that was okay. We had plenty of time to still get to know one another.

And besides, I still didn't have much of an appetite.

I turned to my friends, who were huddled over the notebook, giggling and whispering. "So, what's the plan?"

"We're gonna split up to investigate," Analisa said.

Maya nodded. "I'm gonna see if I can sneak into the hotel where the stars are staying."

"And what are Analisa and I doing?" I asked.

"Go to the theatre to talk to the stagehands," Maya replied.

I pursed my lips together for a moment as I thought about that. "Why can't we go to the hotel?"

Maya smirked. "Because I came up with the plan."

 **CHAPTER 11**

The theatre, which was normally brightly lit and bustling with activity, was nearly empty today. Analisa and I stepped into the back and stared down the empty aisles all the way to the dark stage. Rows and rows of red velour seats stretched up to the front of the house like the red carpet at the Golden Globes.

"Anyone here?" Analisa called out.

I peered into the tech booth at the back of the house. Nobody was in there — just a sound and light board with lots of switches and some headphones.

"Maybe we should come back," I said, turning to leave.

Analisa grabbed my arm. "Come on. Let's take a look around. Maybe we can figure out how the flat fell."

She started off down the aisle, practically dragging me behind her. For someone who supposedly wasn't even into this, she definitely had me fooled. I had to sprint to catch up, my knapsack bouncing on my back with each stride I took. Once again, I wasn't wearing the most practical shoes, but Analisa's were even worse. I looked down at the stiletto sandals she was teetering along on. How could she run in those?

I didn't even think she owned anything like that. I'd never seen her in anything other than dance shoes or flip-flops.

I had to admit that while it wasn't really creepy or anything, I much preferred the theatre when there was an audience filling the seats, especially when they were clapping and cheering me on and throwing bouquets at my feet, of course. But today, not a single noise.

We reached the stage and walked around to the side where a small staircase led up to the stage.

"Hey!" a voice called out from the darkness, as the bright stage lights suddenly flooded the stage, blinding me in the process.

I squinted out into the darkness, but it was impossible to make out who'd just spoken. My eyes still hadn't adjusted to the change in light. But one thing was clear. We weren't alone.

"What are you doing here?" the voice asked.

"Uh—" I stammered.

Analisa hurried up the steps. Once onstage, she stepped forward into the spotlight, smiled brightly, and executed the perfect hair flip. Had she learned that trick from Hadley?

I'd never seen her act like this before. She'd always seemed so quiet.

"I'm sorry," she said in a voice coated with honey. "I didn't realize we couldn't be here. My friend and I are in the cast and we wanted to get used to the stage. You know, before we go live on TV in front of millions of people."

A tall, lanky figure with sandy blond hair and slightly slumped shoulders walked out of the shadows. It was Steve, the stagehand who'd been on duty the night that the flat fell. "You're Analisa, right?"

"Why yes I am," she purred.

What was up with the faux Southern accent? She's from California, for crying out loud. And not even Southern Cali. I tried to catch her eye, but she didn't even look my way. She just focused all her attention on Steve.

And he seemed to be just eating it up. "Sure, no prob. Go right ahead."

Analisa strode confidently to the center of the stage, her hips sashaying with each step. I wish I could do that. I noticed Steve's eyes following her, fixated on the way her leotard and workout shorts clung to her curves. I didn't have enough of a chest to attract that kind of attention.

But Analisa did.

Hmm ... We'd have to use that.

"Um, Ana," I began.

She spun around. "Yeah?"

"Can I talk to you for a minute?"

She smiled in Steve's direction. "Would you excuse me for just a sec?" He nodded.

We walked over to the wings, just off the stage. "What?"

"He likes you," I said. Yup, that's me, Captain Obvious.

Analisa smiled. "Yeah, I think he does."

"Wait a sec. You don't like him, do you?"

She laughed. "I don't even know him. But I think we can make this work for us."

"What should I do?"

She shrugged. "Could you look around while I distract him?"

"I guess so. What am I looking for?"

"Something suspicious. I gotta get back there." She smiled and batted her eyelashes like a modern-day Scarlett O'Hara. "Steve's waiting for me."

Something suspicious ... What the heck did she mean? I wasn't even sure whether she knew herself.

As Analisa flounced back to the center of the stage to flirt with her stagehand, I had a look around backstage. It was a much more technically advanced backstage than what I was used to back home. I couldn't spot a single thing I recognized from the Sparta Middle School auditorium.

I didn't even know what I was looking for. I was a dancer, not a stagehand. The whole extent of my backstage experience was putting on makeup and waiting in the wings before my call.

The contrast between the floodlights of the stage area and the dim lighting backstage was huge. I stubbed my toe and almost tripped over an exposed metal anchor-like contraption jutting up from the floor. I think they called it a shin buster and it's used to tie down sets or something.

I hopped on one foot for a couple of seconds while I rubbed my poor throbbing toe. Ouch!

Wait a second. Tie down sets? Maybe this was what I was

looking for. I wasn't one hundred percent certain of its name, but I was pretty darn sure that's what it was for. It had to be. I might not have been the world's most technically competent gal, but I haven't been completely clueless during the twenty or so performances I've been in over the years.

So was the fallen set Stage Right or Stage Left? I tried to think back to Friday night. Where was it?

"So, Steve" — Analisa's breathy voice cut through the silence — "what do you like to do for fun?"

"Oh, you know ... "

I tuned them out as I tried to remember the get-to-know-you session from a few nights back. Hmm ... We were all sitting in a circle on the stage, and the crash came from ... the right? The left? I decided to check out both sides.

As best as I could tell, nothing looked out of the ordinary, so I moved to the next set piece back. I found the tie-down, but everything seemed to be tied down fine. I silently cursed myself out for not paying more attention to what the technical staff did for our shows.

"Yeah, I love cars," Analisa's voice rang out. "Cars are, like, totally my passion."

She was so full of it. If this whole dancing thing didn't work out, maybe they could find a place for her in the acting program.

I scurried across the narrow passageway behind the upstage area and crossed over to the other side. Stage Right looked nearly identical to Stage Left. I started at the back and figured I'd just make my way downstage.

Once again, I almost tripped over another metal tie-down contraption. I bent down and studied it more closely.

This time, I saw a small piece of cable on the floor next to the shin buster, surrounded by several tiny metal filings that looked like they'd shed off of the cable. They were kind of like rope shreds, only metal.

If only I'd thought to borrow some forensic materials from my mom's colleagues. I laughed as I thought about that conversation. My mom would kill me.

"Do you want to go out some time?" Steve's voice rang out.

Was this where the set piece had been? I closed my eyes and

concentrated on the scene. I'd been on the downstage portion of the circle, facing upstage. My back had been towards the audience and the crash had come from ...

... my left! So that would make it Stage Right, since I was facing the wrong direction. Yes! This could be it.

The cable looked like it had been cut. Even with my untrained eye, I could tell this wasn't just normal wear and tear. I knew that the police had probably combed the whole area but maybe they'd missed some clues. They're trained in CSI, not theatre. How would they know what it should look like? Then again, maybe they hadn't even searched backstage. I hadn't thought twice about the set falling until after the bomb scare yesterday. Maybe they never thought to connect the two events.

If so, maybe the smoking gun, er, I mean, the saw or whatever, was still there. I poked around backstage some more. *If I were a saw or file, where would I be?*

I tried to use some method acting techniques and envision myself as a saw to figure out where I might hide. I felt completely ridiculous, but just when I was about to give up, I came up with the idea to search behind the heavy curtain.

Sure enough, hidden inside the deepest folds of the velvet was a hacksaw of some sort. Now, keeping in mind that the whole extent of my knowledge of tools came from *Extreme Makeover: Home Edition*, I was pretty sure I'd just found my smoking gun.

My suspicions were confirmed — someone was sabotaging the show.

Using the sleeve of my hoodie as a glove, I carefully picked up the saw, taking care not to get my own fingerprints on it. If it was what I thought it was, it could tell the identity of the saboteur. I stashed it in my backpack so I could bring it to the police once I'd amassed more evidence. I knew Mom would kill me if she found out that I was tampering with evidence, but hey, what she didn't know wouldn't hurt her.

FOUND CABLE ON STAGE. LOOKS CUT

I hit send and hoped Maya would respond soon. I didn't want to call attention to my covert position backstage, so I switched the ringer to vibrate.

"Yeah, that's so hot," Analisa cooed in the distance.

At least her tone of voice was completely different from Paris Hilton's.

About a minute later, I felt my phone buzzing in my hand.

WHAT DO U MEAN

I typed back:

SOMEONE CUT TIEDOWN CORD

Buzz ...

IM@HOTEL. HADLEYS HERE

Hmm ... Hadley was at the hotel with the cast? I wondered what she was doing there. We'd been specifically told by Mr. Hawkins that we weren't allowed to go over there except for official cast events. Of course, that didn't stop Maya from sneaking over there to snoop.

I typed back:

WHATS SHE DOIN THERE

Buzz ...

@POOL HANGING ON JMC & NICK

That witch. Didn't she already have a boyfriend?

DID U FIND N E THING

Buzz ...

NO C U BACK @DORM

I stuck the tiny piece of cable in my pocket, and then sauntered back onstage. I tried to act all casual, like I'd been there all along.

"So Steve," I began. "Have the police been around here?"

He jerked his head away from the object of his affection, almost surprised to remember that someone else was there. "Yeah, they have, but they don't think the set falling is related to that other stuff."

"Do you?" I asked.

"Do you?" he retorted, his previously sunny disposition

disappearing. "From what I hear, maybe I should ask you the same thing."

I put my hands up in the air faster than a French soldier in a combat zone. "I had nothing to do with that."

He narrowed his eyes at me. "Yeah, well neither did I."

Analisa stepped forward. "Nobody thinks you did. We're just scared about all this crazy stuff." She leaned in and touched his arm lightly.

Steve puffed out his chest like a Spartan heading into battle at Thermopylae. "I'll protect you, Ana."

I think I threw up in my mouth a little bit.

CHAPTER 12

Back at Ames Hall, we immediately compared notes about our respective investigations. As always, I played secretary and jotted everything down in the official casebook.

"Looks like you guys had a much more productive time than me," Maya said, frowning. "I didn't find anything."

"Sure you did," I said. "You found out that Hadley and her cronies broke Mr. Hawkins' rule and went over to the hotel."

Maya sighed. "Big deal. Like that really means anything."

"Maybe it does mean something," I said, wheels spinning in my brain.

"What?" Maya asked.

"Hadley's spending more time hanging out with the celebrities than with her own boyfriend."

"So what?" Analisa asked.

"It means that Craig might be jealous," Maya said, her dark eyes shining with excitement.

"Most signs do seem to point to him," I said.

"Time out," Analisa interrupted, making a "T" with her hands like a referee. "Craig's a smart guy. He wouldn't risk his career like this."

"Nah," Maya said. "He's doing his best to make people think it's Dani, meanwhile he's trying to discredit the show with that stupid petition. If he can't get it shut down because of the sabotage then he'll just try to shut it down through the legal system."

"How?"

"They're gonna sue."

"But what good does it to do for him if the show is canceled?" Analisa asked.

"I don't know," I admitted. "But maybe he doesn't really want it cancelled. Maybe he just wants to have it opened up to others, like he said."

Analisa glanced at the clock and frowned. "Uh, chicas, I don't mean to break up the party, but we need to run to dinner if we're gonna have time to eat before the costume fitting. We can talk on the way there."

"Yeah, we better get going," I agreed. "And if we're lucky, maybe we'll overhear something."

We left the dorm and walked across campus to the dining hall. One of the weird things about my school was that even if you didn't have a watch, you could tell time just by following the mass exodus across the main quad.

We fell in behind a group of students who'd just left the visual arts building. As we neared the library, I saw a big group of kids holding picket signs, like an anti-war demonstration or labor union strike.

Or something.

"Down with discrimination! Down with discrimination!" they chanted as we approached.

"Give it up," I grumbled under my breath.

A short, somewhat stocky girl with thick-rimmed brown

glasses, about five eyebrow rings, a bracelet tat around her wrist, an Ed Hardy T-shirt, and chunky red streaks in her dyed jet-black hair blocked my path and stuck a petition in my face. Even without looking at it, I knew it had to be the same one Kyle tried to get me to sign earlier.

"Wanna help us change the course of history at this school?" she asked.

Maya shoved the petition back at the girl with such force that she nearly knocked her over. "We're not interested."

The girl's eyes grew wider as she got a better look at us, or rather, at me. "Hey, you're that girl!"

"No, she's not," Analisa snapped, grabbing my arm. "Sorry, but we have to go. It's time for dinner."

"I'm not hungry anymore," I grumbled.

Maya grabbed my other arm and dragged me towards the caf. "Yes you are. Come on."

As we pushed our way through the crowd, I noted, "I have a feeling we're not going to do any better at the dining hall."

"You're probably right," Maya conceded, not able to get around a big knot of kids blocking her way. "Why don't we go to Bangkok Bistro?"

"Oh no." I held up my hands in protest and backed away slightly. "No way am I going there."

"Actually, Dani, we should," Analisa said. "It's a good idea. We could eat and maybe find out a little more info."

"But they put peanut oil in my Pad Thai," I said. "I can't afford to have another allergy attack. The doctor said it wasn't too serious this time but it could be deadly if it happened again."

"There's no way they'd risk it," Maya said. "But if you'd prefer, you can eat at Cantina Mexicana next door. Ana and I can check out Bangkok Bistro."

We made the walk to the strip mall on Main Street in record time. I popped into Cantina Mexicana and ordered a small taco salad, hold the taco, to go. The bright, garish colors and loud Latin music combined to give me such a pounding headache, that when my order was ready, I willingly left to go next door to the Thai place, despite them almost killing me just a few days earlier. At least Bangkok Bistro had the whole feng shui thing going on, with the pleasing décor and soothing colors.

I hadn't even passed the gold-gilded imitation jade Buddha statue when the hostess spotted me. "Oh, you! You okay from other night?"

Guess she recognized me. "Yes, thank you."

She planted her hands on her hips in a defiant posture. "We did not hurt you. We made sure to not use peanuts."

I shrugged. "Well, somehow there was a trace of peanut oil in the food. I had an attack."

The hostess shook her head emphatically. "No. Not from us. We made sure. You are not only customer with allergy. We are very careful."

The cashier, who'd been ringing up their order, looked up as I approached. "You okay?" she asked when she saw me.

"I'm fine," I said, annoyed to keep rehashing the story. I mean, it was nice that they were showing concern, but I just wanted to get on with it.

"I told her we did not use peanuts in Pad Thai," the hostess said.

The cashier nodded. "That is true. We were careful."

"Well, she swelled up like a balloon," Analisa said, stepping in between me and the restaurant workers just like a mother bear protecting her cubs. "So somehow peanuts got in there."

"Not from us," the cashier insisted.

Our little off-campus detour had us running really low on time, so we grabbed our take-out bags and speed-walked across campus to the theatre. We'd have to use this little detour as our warm-up, which was fine with me.

We were definitely getting our heart rates up.

My Grandma Rose taught me about the time of day called "the gloaming," and this was it. The early evening light shown through the leaves of the trees, casting sparkles on the ground between the growing shadows. Normally I loved this magical time of day, but unfortunately I couldn't stop to enjoy it this time.

As we slipped in the back, Mr. Hawkins caught my eye, arched his eyebrow, and shot me a warning look.

I know this was the understatement of the year, but that man did not like me. But, hey, I guess if I were in his shoes, I wouldn't like me much either.

Oh yeah, recipe for disaster, that's me.

One by one, the dressmakers called us back to the dressing rooms for our fittings. They'd measured us during the first rehearsal, so tonight we were trying on what they'd created.

"Daniela Spevak?" a pleasant-looking, plump older woman called out. I shoved my half-eaten salad back in the bag, took a gulp of Diet Coke, and headed for the dressing room, stifling a small burp from chugging the carbonation.

"I'm Harriet Gibson. We're so happy to have you with us. I think you're really going to like your costume, Miss Spevak," she continued, smiling. "It's modest, yet sexy at the same time. Perfect image for this show."

"Can't wait!" I said, mustering up much more enthusiasm than I felt. I liked our jive routine, I really did, but it wasn't anywhere near as cool as Hadley's samba or Analisa's paso doble. The samba's a hot Brazilian street dance popular at Carnival, and the paso doble was the bullfighter's dance. I just knew those routines were going to go over much better than my dorky 1950s nostalgia piece. Then again, beggars couldn't be choosers.

When it came down to it, I was just thrilled to be invited to the party. Hopefully we'd stick around until the second round so the viewers could see our cha-cha.

I followed Mrs. Gibson down the steps to the girls' dressing room. Maya stood in the middle of the room on a dais, being fitted into a slinky little black number with an exposed midriff and lots of fringe. Hadley, dressed in a sparkly hot pink costume, sat at a small vanity behind her, pressing false eyelashes onto her lids. She concentrated on her reflection in a mirror surrounded by many bright light bulbs, like a scene out of a 1940s movie.

I'm ready for my closeup, Mr. DeMille.

"Miss Spevak — may I call you Daniela? — you just stand right over there. Put your stuff down and make yourself at home."

Mrs. Gibson rushed off to the wardrobe at the far edge of the room. "I'm just going to get your costume, dear."

"Hey, Dani," Maya called, barely moving so as not to disturb the dressmaker who was hemming the bottom of the skirt. "What does your costume look like?"

I shrugged. "I have no idea, but Mrs. Gibson says I'm gonna love it."

"Oh, you will, honey!" Mrs. Gibson gushed as she pawed her way through the costumes hanging in the wardrobe. "I made it myself just for your routine, exactly to Ms. McCauley's specifications."

"Do you know what Nick's wearing?" Maya asked.

Hadley spun around, revealing somewhat of a freak-show image. Her left eye had long false eyelashes glued to it, yet her right eye was naked in comparison. "He's gonna look so hot," she said smugly. "All black, and they're slicking his hair back just like an authentic 1950s bad boy, kinda like John Travolta in *Grease*."

"How do you know?" Maya asked.

Hadley smirked. "He showed me yesterday after the meeting."

Oh no, she didn't.

"Where is it?" Mrs. Gibson shrieked. "Oh, no! Where is it?"

"Where is what?" Maya's seamstress asked, looking up with an expression of alarm on her face.

"The costume! Daniela's red jive costume!"

"I saw it on the hanger yesterday evening," the other seamstress said, turning back to her hemming job of Maya's costume. "Look again. It's got to be there."

Mrs. Gibson gestured frantically. "No! I already looked. It's gone! It can't be."

"You'll find it," the other seamstress assured her, not bothering to look up this time.

Mrs. Gibson shook her head. "It's not here."

"Are you sure you left it on that costume railing?" I asked, catching Maya's eye quickly. Maya nodded. She was thinking what I was thinking.

Mrs. Gibson sighed. "I'm absolutely certain. You saw me put it here, didn't you, Marlene?"

Marlene placed her pins in a bright red tomato-shaped pincushion and rushed over to the wardrobe. "Not only did I see you hang it there, but I also saw it there last night."

Maya leaned over to me and whispered, "Last night? Didn't Hadley say she was backstage last night playing with costumes?"

Get out of my head! And once again, it appeared I was the target. No way could it have been a coincidence that my costume went missing.

Marlene picked up a walkie-talkie and barked into it, "Marlene to Command. Marlene to Command. We're missing a costume. Repeat, missing a costume."

Static spouted out of the speaker. "This is Tracy. Please repeat. I think you said you're missing a costume?"

Marlene pursed her lips before responding. "Yes, Miss Spevak's jive costume is missing."

"Did you say Miss Spevak?" The crackle of the bad connection didn't mask Tracy's sigh. "Not again."

A few seconds later, Tracy popped her head into the doorway. "Please tell me I heard wrong."

Mrs. Gibson slumped against the wardrobe. "No. I can't find it."

Tracy looked like she counted to ten before she answered. Maybe she'd done yoga, too. "Okay, well, keep looking for it. We'll just have to do tonight's run-through without it." She turned to face me. "Do you have practice clothes you can wear?" I nodded. "Fine. Wear those for now."

While the other girls slipped into their costumes, I helped Mrs. Gibson root through pieces of clothing, but I never found a bright red jive skirt and top. Crazy as it seemed, the costume really was missing.

Twenty minutes later, they herded us all onstage. Sure enough, I was the only cast member in warm-up clothes. I definitely stuck out like the proverbial sore thumb in my leotard, tights, and artfully ripped sweat pants while everyone else was decked out in sequins and spandex. I'd taken such pains to create the perfect comfy, yet cool, workout attire so I could blend in with the more sophisticated older girls in repertory class, yet now the way too casual clothes only intensified my discomfort.

Man, I couldn't do anything right!

"We'll run through each routine at least four times before moving on to another one. We'll begin with Miss Taylor and Mr. Cooper, then Miss Sapp and Mr. Chen, Miss San Miguel and Mr. Williams, and if we have time, Miss Spevak and Mr. Galliano," Mr. Hawkins said, with a dismissive wave of his hands.

"Why only if we have time?" Nick asked. I had to admit, he did look like John Travolta in his costume.

"Well, Daniela doesn't have a costume, and this *is* a dress rehearsal," Tracy volunteered.

I quickly ran the mental calculation and figured out that it would be at least thirty minutes, if not more, before it was my turn, so I decided to make use of the spare time. Surely, nobody would miss me. And if they did, I could just claim I went to the library. I mean, yeah, this is an arts school, but it's still a *school*. Surely nobody would fault me for my devotion to academics, right?

First stop: Taylor Hall.

CHAPTER 13

I'd never been in the dorm named after Hadley's father before, so I wasn't exactly sure what room I was looking for. Fortunately, just like in Ames, all the rooms had nametags taped to them by the Dorm Mom, a teacher who lives in an apartment on the first floor of each dorm.

The first floor seemed like as good a place as any to begin. The first hall I tried proved unsuccessful, however. As I jogged the length of the corridor, I saw tons of girls' names, but not a single "Hadley Taylor." One down, two more floors to go.

I exited the stairwell into the long hallway of the second floor and immediately began to panic when I spotted a large group of girls at the end of the hall. Technically, as a fellow female student, I had every right in the world to be there, but the covert nature of the mission made me a little nervous. Besides, the last thing I wanted was for someone to recognize me as 'That Girl' and tattle on me to Hadley.

I briefly slipped into the bathroom to try to wait them out and was suddenly overcome by a dizzy spell. The entire room started spinning, and I had to grab hold of the door to one of the stalls to keep myself from falling over. It was weird; one second I was fine and the next, everything went black for a moment. But just for a second. Then I was fine.

Good thing I was stuck in the bathroom and not fainting on the hall floor right out in the open. Talk about embarrassing.

Hopefully they'd just leave. After my watch ticked off three minutes, however, I knew I had to get on with it. I was running out of time if I wanted to check out Hadley's room and then get back before it was my turn to rehearse.

I stepped back into the hall. Thank goodness nobody was around this time.

Huh, whaddya know? The very first suite I came to was marked "Rebecca Bradley, Colleen Davis, Hadley Taylor, Arielle Weinberg."

Now or never.

I glanced furtively around me and saw that it was all clear. I took a deep breath and pushed on the door, just to see whether it was open.

Of course not. That would have been way too easy.

Now what? I couldn't very well not take advantage of my one and only chance to prove once and for all that Hadley was out to get me. I'd have to give up my membership in the *NCIS* fan club if I did.

Wait a sec! I'd just ask myself *WWZD? What would Ziva do?*

Breaking and entering ... but how?

I was just about to send a text to Analisa or Maya when it hit me. Bobby pins! Now that was one thing any dancer had in abundance. I reached up into my hair and pulled a pin out of my bun, then jiggled it into the lock until I heard it click.

Score!

I looked around to get my bearings. First thing I saw was a living room — one couch, one loveseat, one coffee table completely covered with glossy fashion magazines, and a small dining room table with four chairs off in a corner near the window. Stacks of carelessly strewn notebooks and textbooks decorated the table. Not an inch of wood showed. Could've been the perfect spot to find clues, but I skipped it because how exciting could homework really be, you know?

No, if I was going to find anything, it would have to be in the bedroom. I wasn't sure which of the two bedrooms Hadley shared, though. And who was her roommate? But I didn't have much time left, so I decided to just check both rooms out.

I scurried across the living room to the first door I saw and slowly pushed it open.

I was in!

Amazed, yet grateful that Hadley and her friends would leave the door unlocked, I slipped inside and pulled the door closed behind me, taking care not to let it slam. But I guess I shouldn't have been all that surprised. I left my door unlocked that first night, too.

I was momentarily taken aback by the décor, however. While the common area of the suite could easily be mistaken for the room I lived in, the bedroom most definitely could not. Talk about opulence!

I recognized the Calvin Klein bedspread from my parents' master bedroom at home. At one end of the room, I spotted a big-screen flat-panel TV hooked up to a brand-new Wii. An open media cabinet displayed a collection of what appeared to be at least a hundred DVDs, all new releases. Hanging in the tiny closet were rows and rows of expensive-looking clothes that still had the designer hangtags attached. There was even an aquarium of tropical fish against one wall.

I kid you not. Tropical fish.

I had no idea that a simple white institutional room could shape up so nicely, but then again, I guess anything could look like a million bucks if you threw enough money at it.

Had to be Hadley's room. How crazy that her parents lived just a few blocks away, yet they would not only pay for her to live at school, but to decorate her dorm room a thousand times better than any normal kid's bedroom at home.

Now that I was in, I forgot all about why I'd come in the first place. What was I looking for? I didn't really know.

Something … suspicious?

Hadley's amassed collection of stuff would probably be

suspicious in anyone else's room, but her parents' wealth was legendary at the school. That couldn't possibly be my clue.

I spotted a laptop on a desk and thought back to all the crime dramas I'd watched on TV with my mom. The police always found a treasure trove of clues on hard drives. Maybe if I could boot it up ...

"Yeah, he's so hot." A girl's voice interrupted my thoughts. Crap! Were her suitemates back already?

"Oh, I know. Hadley's so lucky to get to hang out with him," another girl said. It sounded like it came from the living room.

How did they get in there without me hearing them?

Okay, so they were talking about Hadley in third person, so chances were, she wasn't around. But still, just because she wasn't there didn't mean that I was safe.

I had to act fast, so I ducked into the open closet and hid behind the long formal gowns. What on Earth was she doing with formal gowns anyway? Was she in the Miss_Teen USA pageant or something?

Wait a minute ... Could she be hiding my costume in here? I glanced around but my eyes hadn't adjusted to the low light inside the closet yet, so I couldn't tell.

I heard a door open and shut. "So what were we supposed to bring?" the first girl asked.

She was in the room. I felt my heart beating so fast I thought I'd drop dead of a heart attack right there. Was that even possible? Couldn't you just imagine the headlines?

GIRL, 15, DIES IN CLASSMATE'S CLOSET

(OK, fourteen ...)

"She wants her dance bag," the second girl answered.

Silence. I couldn't even breathe because I was sure it would be too loud.

"Why doesn't she have it?" the first girl asked. "I thought she was doing the samba tonight?" the first girl asked.

"I don't know. That's just what her message said. She's not answering her cell phone right now. She probably just needs a spare pair."

"Okay."

The voices were getting louder and louder until I realized

they were standing right outside the closet door. I should've known this was the worst idea ever.

"Where does she keep her shoes?"

"Usually her bag is looped on the back of her chair. So I have no clue where to look if it's not there."

"I guess we can try the closet."

Of course.

It was like a bad scene out of a B-grade horror movie. They had to go into the closet, right? Why couldn't I have thrown myself under the bed or something, instead? But of course, with my luck, if I'd done that, then Hadley would need something from under her bed. I just couldn't win. I felt like the too-stupid-to-live teenage girl who always runs towards the killer in those straight-to-DVD flicks. All I needed was a cheerleading uniform and I'd be set.

I heard the knob turn, so I sucked in my breath and squeezed my eyes shut. Maybe they wouldn't see me if I concentrated on being invisible. Right about now would be a nice time for an intervention from a previously unheard of Fairy Godmother.

CHAPTER 14

My throat was so parched I thought I might cough up tumbleweeds and sand. I couldn't believe the other two girls didn't hear the thunderous thumping of my heart. I was pretty sure the volume dial was stuck on high.

Maybe if I clicked my heels together three times and repeated "There's no place like home" then I would be magically transported out of there without being attacked by flying monkeys. No?

Darn.

She can't see me. She can't see me. She can't see me ...

Even through my closed eyelids, I could still sense the stream of brighter light as the door inched open. Ohmygoshohmygoshohmygosh. My spying career cut short before it even began.

I took a breath and opened my eyes, ready to face whatever happened next—

"I found it!" a voice came from across the room.

I heard footsteps getting softer and softer, so I knew they must have been leaving. Their voices were fading away, too, so either I was hallucinating or they'd left the room.

Talk about a close call. Maybe that Fairy Godmother existed, after all. Or at least Glinda the Good Witch. Maybe I should have bought a lottery ticket. Well, if I was old enough, of course.

I knew I had to get out of there. I didn't find what I was looking for, but I couldn't take any more chances.

But I also couldn't risk stepping out into the open just yet.

I waited another minute or so, and then I poked my head out the closet door. The coast was clear, so I bolted as fast as I could and didn't stop until I got outside into the fresh air.

I sneaked back into the auditorium amidst the roar of applause for Hadley and JMC, and slipped into a seat in the house next to Maya.

"What did I miss?"

"Me. And I rocked." Maya laughed. "We're gonna totally win."

"He didn't call me, did he?"

"Nah. He hasn't even gotten to Ana yet."

As if on cue, Mr. Hawkins' baritone boomed, "Miss San Miguel and Mr. Cooper?"

A lone guitar wailed as Spanish flamenco music filled the theatre. Daronn made a dramatic entrance, carrying Analisa high above his head. A scowl marred his normal boyish good looks. Even though he wasn't an actor, he did a better job of transforming himself into his character than Nick. Gone was the hip hop star, utterly replaced by the most masculine example of macho culture — the matador.

Analisa wore a slinky lace bodice with a long red skirt. She slid down his arm and when her feet were firmly planted on the floor, she gazed deeply into his eyes. Wow — talk about intense!

I quickly glanced at Tracy, sitting across the room next to her boss. Mr. Hawkins looked transfixed, but Tracy looked like she was about to blow a gasket. Probably had something to do with the overly sensual display onstage.

Guess we'd better brace ourselves for a Focus on the Family protest. I wonder what the advertisers would think?

Onstage, Daronn took Analisa's hand in his and spun her out, leaving her skirt in his hands. She confidently stepped away, revealing a skimpy lacy red and black costume. He waved the skirt-turned-cape over his head like a lasso as Analisa leapt across the stage towards him. As the music swelled to a crescendo, he grabbed her hands and they began the classic steps of the paso doble, their heels clicking on the floor as fast and as loudly as castanets.

Daronn spun her towards him and lifted her easily off the floor. Everyone applauded and whistled. Damn they were good. And judging from the expression on Daronn's face, he knew it.

Oh yeah, he knew it.

"Put me down!" Analisa suddenly wailed.

Her partner was so startled he nearly dropped her, but he complied. Once she was on the ground, Analisa ran off the stage in tears, clutching the front of her costume.

"What's wrong?" Mr. Hawkins' voice bellowed throughout the quiet theatre.

From behind the curtain, we could hear Analisa sobbing. Marlene, the assistant seamstress who'd been fitting Maya earlier, stepped out of the wings.

"Her straps — they've been cut!" she said, her voice tinged with distress.

We all rushed backstage to see our friend. Analisa was showing Tracy that the lace straps, which had just a minute ago been holding up the costume, were broken.

"I can't believe I was up onstage like that." A pinched expression crossed Analisa's face. "It's so embarrassing."

"Couldn't they just have ripped?" Tracy asked.

Mrs. Gibson straightened up and shook her head, a deep crease forming in her forehead. "No. That's a clean cut on the material. See that little thread there? It looks like someone sewed them back on ... rather sloppily, I might add. I would never let any of my staff do such shoddy work."

Tracy pursed her lips together. "Fine. The dress rehearsal is canceled. We'll just do it as it gets closer to filming."

Mr. Hawkins rubbed his temples as he nodded. "Please go back to your rooms and get a good night's sleep. Come back tomorrow ready to work. We cannot afford to have any more problems."

We walked Analisa back to Ames Hall. She was still upset but had regained her composure.

Just barely.

"If I hadn't asked Daronn to put me down I would've flashed everyone! What if it happened when we were live?"

"I think that was actually the intention," I said.

"Kinda gives the term 'wardrobe malfunction' new meaning," Maya joked.

"Not funny," Analisa grumbled, although I detected the hint of a smile.

"So, do you think it was deliberate?" I asked.

"Absolutely," Maya said. "Mrs. Gibson said it was a clean cut and then just tacked back together quickly. Someone wanted that costume to fall apart. I think it just fell apart sooner than expected."

"Probably the same person who stole my costume," I groused.

Analisa stopped abruptly. "Can we please stop talking about the case?" she asked. "I'm tired and just want to go to bed."

We all nodded and kept our mouths shut for the rest of the way back to the dorm.

Instead of relaxing in the commons room, Analisa marched straight to her own room. Maya shrugged and followed her, so I went to my room.

Bev was in her customary spot, huddled over her laptop, her art supplies dumped in a messy pile on her bed. Did she ever leave? It seemed like she was always surfing the Internet. I considered saying "hi," but really, what was the point? Instead, I buried myself in the tiny closet and started changing out of my leotard and into pajamas.

That's when it hit me.

"Thanks Bev!" I called as I ran out of the room. She didn't even bother looking up.

I banged on Maya's door. "Why don't we do some Internet research on our suspects' backgrounds?" I asked when she opened up.

A wide grin spread across her face. "Why didn't I think of that?"

We went to her desk and she booted the computer.

"OK, we need a list of suspects," I said, curling up on Maya's bed with a blanket and pillows. "I guess we should start with the most likely ones."

"Craig and Hadley?" Maya asked.

I nodded. "Who else?"

Maya's fingers flew on the keyboard. She opened up Google, typed in "Craig W," and then stopped. "How do you spell Craig's last name?"

"W-A-S-H-O-S-K-Y," Analisa answered, entering the room. She wore light pink Victoria's Secret PJ's with her hair pulled away from her face in a messy bun.

I bounced over to her and threw my arms around her neck, hugging her tightly. I was so glad she felt better. "I thought you didn't want anything to do with the case anymore."

She shrugged. "If whoever damaged my costume did these other things, I'd be stupid not to get involved. I mean, yeah, it would've been embarrassing if everyone saw my boobs, but they didn't. Arson, on the other hand, is a serious crime. We can't let whoever did that get away with it."

"So you think Craig's responsible?" I asked, pulling up a chair for Analisa and returning to the computer.

"Maybe."

We all peered at the screen, as a relatively short hit list came up, mostly press releases about the various plays Craig had been in while at the arts school.

"How promising is he?" I asked.

"What do you mean?"

"As an actor."

"Well, he's the best male actor at the school," Maya answered. "But in comparison with other young actors across the country? I have no idea."

I grabbed the mouse away from Maya and clicked on a story about Craig's award-winning performance as Curly in *Oklahoma*. "Didn't you say something about Yale?"

"Yeah, he has an audition coming up for their drama program," Analisa said.

I surfed back to the hit list and scrolled down until I came to a link marked "Yale Drama Program." I clicked on it and it brought us to a schedule of some sort. The top of the page was labeled "Auditions."

"Looks like he already went," I said. According to this website, Craig was in New Haven this past weekend for an audition on Saturday afternoon.

"I knew he had nothing to do with this," Analisa said, rubbing her hands together. "He wasn't anywhere near here when the bomb and the fire happened."

"Not so fast," Maya said, taking the mouse away from me. "Just because he has an alibi for that time period doesn't mean he isn't involved."

"But he wasn't even here," I said.

Maya shrugged. "He could have an accomplice."

"No way is Tim involved," Analisa said.

"Does he have an alibi?" I asked.

Maya's face lit up. "Let's check." The keys clacked as she typed in "Tim Wong." This time, many more hits came up, and it appeared that the overwhelming majority of them weren't the Tim we wanted.

"Forty-three million hits? We're gonna be here all night!" Analisa cried, slumping back against her chair.

"Try all week," Maya corrected.

"Why don't we split up the research? That would make it go much quicker," I said.

"Yeah, okay," Analisa agreed. "Makes no sense for us all to look over Maya's shoulder."

We split up the names and each went back to our rooms. I sat down in front of my desk. As the computer screen registered the boot sequence, my cell phone rang. I glanced down at the tiny screen.

Nick!

"Hey," I said.

"Hey yourself. That was weird about your costume, wasn't it?"

"Yeah. But I'm sure Mrs. Gibson just misplaced it."

"Of course. So, what are your plans for tomorrow night?"

Tuesday night ... only thing on TV was *NCIS*. My fave, but I could totally catch it on DVR. "Probably just catching up with my homework. I'm totally going to flunk Geometry if I don't get to studying."

"Oh, well I thought maybe we could go out to dinner and get to know one another better."

Nick wanted to get to know me better! *Deep breath, Dani, deep breath.* "Sure, we could do that."

"Alone this time." He laughed. "Sorry JMC and Hadley tagged along last time. That definitely wasn't my idea."

"No Bangkok Bistro this time," I joked.

His warm infectious laughter poured out of the phone. "How does Italian sound? I found this really cool place around the corner from my hotel."

Italian? I couldn't exactly eat anything on the menu. Too many carbs. Not to mention calories. Ugh.

"Sounds great."

We chatted some more and then made plans for him to pick me up at seven, so that I'd have time to get some homework done before our date. Well, he didn't call it a date, but obviously that's what it was.

I just had to tell Whitney.

"Hello?" my sister's voice answered.

"Hey Whit."

"Dani! So, what have you found?"

"Well, Craig was in New Haven the day of the bomb and the fire, so he couldn't have done it, but we think his friend Tim might have. He's a stagehand, so he would've had access to the set flat. Means and opportunity."

"What's the motive?"

"I don't know."

Whitney sighed. "Haven't you paid attention to any of

mom's cases? There's always a motive."

"Jealousy?"

"Too obvious."

"Well, anyway, Whit, that wasn't why I was calling."

"Okay, what's up?"

"Guess who I'm going out on a date with?" I paused dramatically. Where was my drumroll? "Nick Galliano."

"No way!"

"He just asked me to dinner. Beat that, Whit!"

"You have all the luck!"

I giggled. Definite role reversal. "I know."

"So, what did your background check of him show?"

"Oh, we haven't checked him out, but there's no need to. We already know it was Tim and Craig."

CHAPTER 15

I skipped yoga the next morning so Nick and I could practice the jive routine. As I walked into the studio, I thought about what Whitney had said. I guess I needed to check out his background, too.

Standard operating procedure, of course.

Later. Right now, I had him all to myself.

"I'll be so glad once we get to move onto a new dance," Nick said as he lunged forward to stretch out his quads.

I laughed as I extended my leg on the barre. "I know what you mean. Jive is fun, but I want to do the paso. Did you see that routine last night?"

"Yeah, that was pretty cool." He strode over to the barre and imitated my stretch, which made me giggle because he couldn't quite reach his leg up there. "But I want to do the rumba."

I bent over my leg. "Why?"

He gave up on the stretch and came up right behind me, lightly holding me around my waist. "Because it's way more sensual. I'd really like to dance that with you."

I straightened up and met his intense gaze in the mirror. I could feel a hot blush sweep my body and turned away.

"No really, Dani." I felt his warm breath on the back of my neck. "The dance of love. I think we'd totally kill that one." He leaned in closer, his lips just inches from my skin. "I wouldn't even have to act."

"I thought the bolero was the dance of love," I whispered, turning my head so I could see him.

"No, it's the rumba." How'd he know that? "And it's just oozing with sensuality."

It felt like thousands of tiny raindrops were lightly tickling my body. What was wrong with me? I'd never felt like that before. But I had to admit. It was nice.

Really nice.

"Um, don't we need to practice?" I asked, barely above a whisper. I didn't really want to break the intense connection, but I didn't know what else to do.

His radiant smile lit up the room with its warmth. "Sure." He walked to the center of the room and got into position.

"Just a second," I said. I grabbed my ballroom shoes out of my bag and pulled them on. "Okay."

As I pushed "play" on the remote control, I noticed that he mouthed the word "tonight."

"You okay?" he asked when I missed my cue, immersed in a dream world, like I was walking on clouds.

A movie star wanted to rumba with me! And not just any movie star, but an older guy. He was seventeen! More Whitney's age than mine, yet he chose me. Me! And we were going on a date tonight.

Alone.

I just knew he liked me!

"Uh, yeah," I stammered. "Sorry. I was just a little distracted. Can we try it again?"

The door opened and Tracy stuck her head into the studio. "Hey guys," she said. "I heard you weren't in yoga, so I thought you might be rehearsing. Hope you don't mind if I watch?"

"Come on in," Nick invited.

"Am I in trouble?" I asked.

Tracy walked over to the stool at the front of the room. "What for?"

"I skipped yoga."

She shrugged as she sat down. "They'll get over it. Just don't skip an academic class or any of your actual dance classes.

But yoga is probably fine."

Nick got into position and we tried it again from the top, this time with an audience. As we got into character — him a greaser and me a bobbysoxer — I thought again about how he said he wouldn't have to act if we did the rumba.

How exciting! I couldn't wait until we switched dances. We'd just have to make it past the first round, and then maybe I could talk Tracy into rigging it so we got the rumba next.

I skipped over to my partner and he spun me around. But this time I lost my footing and fell flat on my butt. Sure, I'd fallen before when the cameras were around, but those were planned.

"Are you okay?" Tracy asked, jumping up and sprinting to my side.

"Yeah," I said, a little shaken. "I'm fine."

"What happened?" Nick asked.

"I don't know. It felt like I was on ice or something."

Tracy knitted her skinny penciled-on brows. "Ice?"

"Or something. It was really slick."

Nick crouched down and felt his hand over the floor. "It's not wet."

Tracy peered down at the soles of my ballroom shoes. "Dani, why haven't you been using your shoe brush?"

"I have."

Mr. Hawkins had taught us that ballroom dancers needed to keep the suede bottoms of their shoes in top form. The suede needed to be brushed so that it provided the right traction on the floor. The floor polish of hardwood floors created an oily build-up on the suede if you didn't brush it, and that slick surface could be dangerous. I took that warning to heart and had been religiously brushing my shoes whenever I got the chance.

"You couldn't have been. Your soles are as shiny as a baby's butt. No wonder you fell."

I unstrapped my heels and held them upside down so I could inspect the soles. Sure enough, the suede was matted down and a sticky substance covered the surface, forming a shiny, slippery bottom. I turned them over and looked closer at the delicate satin straps.

"These aren't my latin shoes," I finally said.

Yes they are," Nick said. "I saw you pull them out of your bag."

"No, they're not. My latin shoes have crisscrossed straps. These straps are a sunburst pattern."

Tracy picked up one of the shoes and examined it. "She's right. See this shank?" She pointed to the molded instep between the ball of the shoe and the heel area. "I specifically chose shoes with an adjustable ankle strap that shoots up from the shank, providing additional support. I don't like the idea of such young girls dancing in high heels, but Mr. Hawkins insisted, so I picked the safest ones I could find."

Nick frowned. "Are you sure?"

"Absolutely," Tracy answered. "They're not even the right brand." She looked at me. "Where did you get these?"

I shrugged. "They were in my dance bag. I didn't really pay attention. I just assumed they were my shoes."

She straightened up, clutching the dance shoe in her hands. "Well, Dani, you're lucky. You could've been really injured. It looks like someone specifically switched your shoes. I guess they took 'break a leg' a little too literally."

CHAPTER 16

On my walk back to Ames Hall, I passed more protestors. It was becoming a fixture of my day. I found it funny that they really thought the American Civil Liberties Union would take up their case.

Hilarious!

Speaking of a case, something niggled at the back of my brain. What was I missing? I felt like the solution was staring me right in the face, yet I just couldn't figure it out.

I needed to talk to my girls. Maybe I could bounce some ideas off them and together we could solve it.

I texted them to let them know I was on my way. Maya said they were in Analisa's room. When I got upstairs, I quickly filled them in about the damaged dance shoes. Maya, who'd been lounging on one of the beds with a dog-eared copy of *Pride and Prejudice*, jumped up suddenly.

"Nick!"

"You're crazy," I said, taking a step back.

Maya shook her head frantically. "No, I'm not. He was there when the set fell—"

"So were we," I countered.

"—and was in the studio with you so he could've planted the bomb in your bag. And he was at the restaurant when you got sick and who knows where he really was during the party when the fire was set. And didn't Hadley say they were looking at costumes the other night?"

Analisa took a long sip of soda before answering. "She has a point, Dani."

"No way."

Analisa walked over to me, put her arm around my shoulders, and squeezed lightly. "I know you like him a lot, Dani."

"No." I wiggled my way out of her hold and collapsed onto the twin bed furthest away from the door. "You're wrong."

Analisa walked over and sat down next to me. "Just because you have a crush on him doesn't mean he couldn't do these things."

"I don't have a crush on him!" I protested. Okay, so that was totally a lie, I know. But they were really pissing me off with that line of questioning. "And besides, I've helped my mom with lots of cases and the one thing she's drilled into my head is that you need a motive. 'Find the motive and you've found your perp.' Motive, means, and opportunity, that's what you need. What possible motive would Nick have?"

Maya shrugged. "What motive does anyone have to sabotage the show?"

"Craig has a really big motive," I said "He wants to discredit some of the people on the show, so they'll have to put him on instead."

"But he wasn't even around when the bomb appeared," Analisa said. "He was at the Yale audition."

I curled myself into a ball. "Tim was here, though."

"She's right. Nick doesn't have a motive, but Craig does. And so does Hadley," Maya added. "She'd have a much easier time winning if you were gone, Dani."

"Have you checked out her background?" I asked.

"Not yet," Maya admitted.

"I'll do it," I offered. "Can I use your computer, Ana?"

"Only if you also check out Nick," she replied.

I stuck out my tongue at her after that last remark. Juvenile, yes, what could I say? I sat down at the desk. The screen was in sleep mode, so I jiggled the mouse to get it to spring to life. I closed her IM session and found a Google hitlist about Analisa's own partner, Daronn Williams.

"So did Daronn do it?" I asked.

Analisa laughed. "Not that I know of."

I typed "Nick Galliano" in the search engine and pulled up a laundry list of articles about his movies and the latest celebutantes he'd been spotted with. I hated to admit it, but I felt a twinge of jealousy when I read about his dating exploits. But just for a second. *I* was the one going out with him tonight. Not Demi Lovato, not Abigail Breslin.

Me.

"See?" I said. "Just a list of movies. I told you he didn't do it."

I was gloating just a little (okay, a lot) when I closed the browser. Without it on the screen, Analisa's other web browser popped open to WebMD.

"Do you feel okay?" I asked her. If she was coming down with a cold then I needed to get out of there, because I definitely couldn't afford to get sick now.

"Yeah, why?"

I pointed at the screen. "You were looking at WebMD."

Analisa jumped up from the floor and headed my direction. "I'll take over."

But before she could push me out of the chair, I caught a glimpse of the medical articles she'd been reading.

"Anorexia & Bulimia"

"Body Image & Disordered Eating"

"Eating Disorders: Fact or Fiction?"

"Eating Disorders: Recognizing the Warning

Signs"

"Wannarexia: Wishing You Had an Eating

Disorder"

And the kicker?

"What To Do If Your Friend Has an Eating

Disorder"

"What the—?"

I spun in the chair and searched the girls' faces for an answer. Oh, I got it, all right. Loud and clear.

They thought I had an eating disorder. As if!

My friends wouldn't even look me in the eye. Analisa's cheeks were turning a shade darker than my Mom's diamond-and-ruby anniversary band, and Maya ate off all her Raspberry Perfection lip gloss as she gnawed on her lower lip.

They thought I was like one of those crazy model chicks who starved themselves to fit into a size 0, didn't they?

"What *is* this?" I demanded.

"Uh," Analisa stammered.

"These WebMD articles. What's this all about?" I asked.

Maya raised her hands in defense. "She was just trying to help."

"Help?" I squeaked. "Who needs help?"

Analisa pursed her lips before answering. "We're worried about you."

Unreal.

"Worried about me?" My voice was nearing that super-high pitch range that humans can't hear, and only dogs can. "What's there to worry about?"

"Well, you get cold or dizzy a lot, and that can be a sign of anorexia," Analisa said, her fingers laced in a death grip on the back of her chair. "And you skip breakfast and lunch most of the time, and then just eat a salad for dinner."

"I eat!"

Maya shook her head. "Barely."

"You have no idea what you're talking about," I said, standing up and backing away from them. "No idea. I'm just trying to watch my weight."

Why didn't they understand? They were dancers. They knew what it was like. Surely they'd seen girls get taken out of routines because they'd gained weight. Certainly they'd worried about not fitting into the costumes.

It's like in that musical, *A Chorus Line*. You ever heard that song "Dance: 10, Looks: 3"? It's about this chick who auditions for shows but never gets a part because she's not cute enough. Every dancer's nightmare.

They had to understand. They had to.

"It's dangerous," Maya said.

Analisa nodded, her normally shining eyes dark. "When I was twelve, I was an understudy in *Gaite Parisienne*—"

"Well, whoop-de-doo for you," I said, balling my hands into fists.

"Let me finish!" Analisa finally looked me in the eye. "I was an understudy, and I didn't think I'd get to dance in the show, but at the last minute, I did. You know why?" She placed her hands on her hips and squared off. "Because one of the older girls ended up in the hospital. And she didn't break her leg, and she sure as heck didn't have a piece of the set fall on her head." She paused. "She weighed only eighty-eight pounds. She was sick, Dani. And she got that way because she thought she needed to 'watch her weight.'"

"What, so you think I stick my finger down my throat or something?" I pushed the chair for emphasis. "I don't puke."

"Nobody said you did," Maya began.

"I'm fine!" I yelled.

"I'm sure Rachel thought she was fine, too," Analisa said.

"Whatever."

Maya stepped between us. "Dani, don't get mad at Ana. She's just—"

"I'm mad at you, too!"

"—worried about you." She held her arms out, as if to hug me. "I am, too."

"Get away from me." I pushed my way to the door. I didn't

need this.

I didn't need them!

"Dani, wait!"

I could hear them calling out for me, but I didn't care. What the heck did they think? I didn't have an eating disorder. Like they really knew anything.

They were so stupid.

I could solve the mystery all by myself. And I was going to win the contest. And I'd go on my date with Nick and they'd be jealous.

That had to be what this was about. They were jealous of me.

Jealous.

Of me!

They were jealous because Nick Galliano liked me, and not them. They were no better than Hadley.

Whatever. I didn't need them.

I left the dorm and stalked towards the studios. I had to be missing something. And I was going to find it. I was going to solve this case. I'd show them.

They were so dumb, like really dumb, for real. There was nothing wrong with my eating. I was just trying to stay in shape. How was that a problem?

It wasn't. If anything, it was admirable. With obesity rates on the rise in this country, I should be applauded for my efforts, not yelled at.

It was just starting to get dark as I passed the stage door of the theatre. A light was on inside, and the silhouettes on the shade suggested a rehearsal going on. Probably *You Can't Take it With You*. Guess I wasn't going to get to snoop in there.

That was fine. I'd already found the file in the theatre. No need to do anything else there. But I needed to get a closer look at the studio that had been set on fire. I wasn't sure what to look for, so I was just hoping I'd know it when I saw it.

I was still fuming from my confrontation with Analisa and Maya and almost didn't hear the footsteps behind me.

Wait, did I hear anything? I whipped around only to discover nobody was there. Duh, it was a campus. There were people around all the time. It was probably just a student entering the library.

Determined not to let my overactive imagination get the better of me, I continued marching towards Vladirov Studio. There was nobody out there. Nobody out there. I just had to remember that.

Only this time I was sure I heard something.

I started to turn around to check, when all of a sudden everything went dark. No, this isn't one of those action movies where someone clunks the heroine on the head and she goes unconscious and then wakes up in a strange room somewhere. Actually, all the streetlamps just turned off. At the same time.

What the—

Wow, it was dark. Was it later than I thought?

I had to admit it was kind of creepy being there all by myself in the dark. My arms were prickling. And it wasn't like I even knew what I was looking for anyway, so I decided to turn around and head back to the dorm. Maybe I could come back with Nick later. He'd probably know what to look for.

I know I'd promised the girls I wouldn't tell him, but it wasn't like I really cared what they thought anyway.

A few minutes later I reached my room and slammed the door behind me. The loud noise caused Bev to look up for a second before she returned to her computer game.

Yeah, I know. Hell had clearly frozen over.

I threw myself down on my bed and stared up at the ceiling.

I couldn't believe they thought I had an eating disorder! That didn't even make any sense. I ate all the time. Sometimes. When I remembered, at least. I mean, didn't everyone skip meals from time to time?

I just needed to watch my weight. At dinner this past weekend, Hadley said my body sucked, but she was going to be sorry. I'd show her.

I'd show them all.

I was just watching my weight, that's all. And I was going to be H-O-T when I went on TV. Couldn't my friends see that?

"It's totally normal to skip meals sometimes, isn't it?" I asked my roommate.

"No."

She speaks! Wait, that wasn't the answer I was looking for.

I sat up straight and stared at my resident goth-girl. For once, she wasn't typing. She was actually looking back at me.

And she looked, I don't know, concerned. Or as concerned as Bev Marcus actually can look, given her status as an apathetic urban rebel and all.

She bit her lower lip, like she wanted to say something, but also didn't want to. I could tell she was totally fighting it.

"What do you mean?" I asked, waiting for the silence, which I got. For two whole minutes.

"My older sister was a dancer," she finally said in a tiny voice.

"*Was* a dancer?"

"She's dead." A lone tear streaked its way down her cheek, ruining her heavy black eye makeup as she spat out the words. "She thought she was fat, so she started losing weight until she finally starved herself to death."

"But it's just a couple of lunches," I said in a whisper.

"That's what she thought, too!" She blinked. "That's how it starts. Just a couple of lunches. And that becomes just a couple of breakfasts. Then just a couple of dinners. She swore she could stop at any time. Yeah, she stopped all right. She stopped eating altogether. And all just because she thought she was two pounds overweight. Now I never get to see her again!"

I had no idea. I stepped forward, wanting to reach out and hug her, but I stopped short, afraid of what she might say. Despite this glimpse of vulnerability, Bev didn't exactly seem like the kind of girl who hugged.

"Um," I started.

She shook her head. "Whatever." And she turned back to her computer, wiping the tears away from her eyes.

Maybe they were right. Maybe I was putting myself in danger.

That's when I made the pledge. I was going to be healthy. And I was going to start tonight at dinner. With Nick.

Oh, shoot! Dinner! I stole a quick look over Bev's shoulder. I only had twenty minutes before I had to meet him. And I was a wreck!

I ran to the bathroom and stripped out of my dance clothes. But before I could jump into the shower, I caught a glimpse of myself in the mirror.

I was skinny.

Not like scary Ellen-Pompeo-skinny or anything, but I definitely didn't need to lose weight. What the heck was I thinking?

I needed to make a change. I mean, it's not like I wanted to gain weight, but I definitely didn't need to lose it.

And besides, I danced forty hours a week. I got way more exercise than most girls, so why was I crash dieting?

It would be hard, but I would not skip any more meals. It wasn't worth it.

After the quickest shower ever, I threw on a short teal halter dress with black high heel sandals. I carefully applied some lip gloss and just a touch of mascara, then blew out my hair so it hung in soft waves down my back.

I spun around to model for Bev. "How do I look?"

Not surprisingly, she didn't bother to look up, let alone answer, which was kinda sad, given what we'd just shared. But really, what did I care? I had a date with Nick!

I grabbed my Coach purse. "Don't wait up."

CHAPTER 17

Dinner was fan-freakin-tastic. Who knew carbs could taste so good?

I'd never been to Pomodoro before, but I was pretty sure it would quickly become a favorite. For an appetizer, we split an order of calamari and fried zucchini in a marinara dipping sauce. Next, I had sautéed shrimp in a garlic tomato sauce with sun-dried tomatoes, roasted red peppers, and chunks of fresh mozzarella over angel hair pasta. Oh, it was heaven. Ooey, gooey, garlicky yum.

Nick suggested we split an order of tiramisu, but I passed. It looked amazing, don't get me wrong, but this was more food than I'd eaten in a really long time, and I was stuffed.

Baby steps.

When we finally left, I thought Nick would have to roll me out the door, which would be really embarrassing, but when I thought back to the spectacular flavors, I just didn't care. I was worth it.

My friends were right. Food was good.

"Thanks for dinner," I said as we walked towards campus.

"I was glad to see you enjoy your food for once." He smiled. "So what do you wanna do now?"

"Well, it's a school night, so I kinda have to do some homework."

He placed his hands on my shoulders and faced me square on with a plaintive look in his eyes. "Dani, it's way too early to go home."

"Um, I guess I could stay a little bit longer," I said, mental wheels spinning as I tried to figure out how I would get my darn geometry finished.

Hold the presses. What was I thinking? There I was, on a date with the hottest guy in the entire world, and all I could think about was the square root of the hypotenuse of the whatchamacallit?

I had to get my head checked.

"Sure," I said more confidently, trying to mimic the breathy tone of voice I'd heard Analisa use around Steve the day before. "We can hang out."

"How does a stroll in the gardens sound?"

A stroll? Wow, that sounded so grown-up. Most guys I knew walked or ran rather than strolled. But Nick wasn't "most guys."

Oh, no, he wasn't!

"Great," I whispered with a smile.

As we strolled along, he surreptitiously inched his left hand closer and closer to my right one until he finally grabbed it and squeezed lightly. His hand was soft, yet rough at the same time, and comfortably warm.

I'd held his hand many times in partnering class, but somehow, this was different.

And boy was it nice.

Finally, we came to the entrance to the Albert P. Walker Memorial Gardens, the most beautiful part of campus. I'm still not completely sure who Albert P. Walker was — I think he was our founder's third *and* fifth husband — but who cares? It was really hard not to like a several-acre plot of land that had been cultivated with thousands of lilies, roses, and cacti.

From what I understood, on a clear spring day, the gardens were full of students sunbathing, studying, practicing Shakespeare scenes, and painting. But tonight it was empty. Just me and Nick.

Aw, yeah.

The pink threads of sunset were long gone and the nighttime was beginning to cast a shadow over the gardens. It wasn't totally dark yet, though. In fact, the lights hadn't even come on and the moon hadn't yet appeared. I glanced down at my watch to see what time it was. Eight-forty-five. I had forty-five minutes before curfew. No problem.

"So, do you think you want to go college, or do you want to just make more movies instead?" I asked, breaking the silence. "Not that that's a 'just make more movies,' 'cuz it's not like I could make movies, but ... " I trailed off, because I knew I was babbling.

He lightly caressed my lips with his finger, sending a shiver through my body unlike anything I'd ever felt. "Don't talk," he said.

"Why?" I whispered.

He gestured broadly at the Southwestern landscape like he was a director on a movie set. "We don't want to ruin this."

I felt a hot flush in my cheeks and was glad it was dark. "Why not?" Was he going to do what I thought he was going to do?

He brushed a strand of hair from my face and gazed at me again with those intense brown eyes. "Because it's beautiful, and you're beautiful, so everything's perfect just as it is."

He thinks I'm beautiful!

He took my hand in his again and we continued to stroll along in silence towards the gazebo, a favorite spot of campus couples. I climbed the steps and followed him inside. He sat down on the bench and pulled me towards him. From our vantage point, sitting side-by-side, we had an unobstructed view of the famous Camelback Mountain.

We sat in silence for a few minutes, just watching the scenery as the night descended on us. He slowly dropped my hand and inched his arm up my own until it draped my shoulders. I could feel tingles all over my body as I snuggled into the space between his arm and his body. A perfect fit!

"This is beautiful," I said.

"Dani, don't talk."

And with that, he finally did it! He lightly grazed my cheek with his fingertips and turned my face towards him. He pulled me in, wrapped his arms around my shoulders and kissed me.

It happened so fast that I didn't even have time to prepare myself, despite the fact that I'd been waiting for this very moment all week. But when he did, all my nervous anticipation melted away and I knew I could do this forever and never grow bored.

My first real kiss!

I mean, yeah, sure, I'd kissed Andrew Burdette at Sophie Roth's bat mitzvah in seventh grade, but that didn't count. Not really. That was slimy and awkward and weird.

This was the real thing.

You know how some people say they see fireworks? I'd always thought that was just a stupid cliché and physically impossible anyway. And now I can say for certain that it's not true.

No, I definitely liked it. Don't get me wrong. But there were no rockets lighting up the sky or anything. Not that it really mattered, because this? Well, it's so very much more. I can't even begin to put into words what I was experiencing all over my body. It was so magical, so powerful, so perfect.

Okay, yeah, it was a little weird, too. But in a good way.

Finally, he pulled away and gazed at me.

"Do that again," I whispered.

But I didn't give him the chance. This time I leaned in and kissed him right back. Slow and tentative at first, as I felt my way around. Then stronger and with more urgency, until I felt the electricity all the way down to my toes.

He definitely knew what he was doing better than Andrew Burdette.

I totally lost track of the time, and what a great way to do that. I didn't ever want to stop, but unfortunately, I had to pee.

Stupid bladder.

I excused myself, promised to be right back, and snuck off to the little public restroom at the edge of the garden.

I'd just been kissed by Nick Galliano!

Now I know it's extremely uncool to kiss and tell, but I just couldn't help it. I had to tell someone, and I didn't want to wait until I got back to the dorm. So I pulled my cell phone out of my purse and dialed Whitney. We've always shared everything. It would be wrong to hold back on this.

"Dani? What's up?"

"Guess what? Nick kissed me!"

She squealed on the other end of the line. "Is he a good kisser?"

"Mmm ... "

"Oh no. You're not getting off that easily." Her musical laughter trickled through the line, forcing me to smile despite myself. "That's so cool, Dani. Oh, and guess what? I found out some really good news about Nick."

That definitely sounded promising. I knew he couldn't have been involved!

"What?"

"It sounded like you weren't going to bother checking his background, so I did." Whitney paused. "Well, I just found out that Nick's going to get the lead in a new football movie called *First Down*. The contract's worth seven million dollars!"

"Dani?" Speaking of Nick, his voice called out from the darkness outside. "Are you still in there?"

"Is that him?" My sister sounded like an excited little girl. "Where are you?"

"In the bathroom at the gardens. Sorry, Whit," I whispered into the phone. "I better go. I'll call you later."

A sharp rap at the door startled me and I dropped the phone into my purse. I turned on the water, not to rinse my hands, but because I was embarrassed that he might have heard my conversation. How long had he been at the door? I would just die if he'd heard me telling Whitney about the kiss.

I mean, yeah, it was wonderful, and I didn't mind him knowing that, but I didn't want him to know it was my first kiss. He didn't need to know how inexperienced I was.

Finally, I toweled off my hands, quickly straightened my hair in the mirror, and then exited the small building. He was standing just outside the door, leaning against the wall, smiling at me.

"Hey."

"Hey," I echoed.

"Who were you talking to?" he asked, his eyebrows raised.

"Uh, nobody?" I said, my voice turning up in a question

despite my best efforts at fibbing.

"Oh, okay." He didn't quite look like he believed me, but didn't say anything else about it. "It's almost nine-thirty, so we better turn around and get you back to your dorm."

I forced myself to smile, despite the fact that going home was about the last thing on my mind. I bet none of the heiresses he met in clubs had curfews. For the first time ever, I mentally cursed myself for all my school's rules. Sure, I had way more freedom here than back in Sparta, but it had to be stricter than a movie set.

Movie sets ... My heart did the cha-cha when I thought of his lead role. Was he keeping it as a surprise? When was he planning on telling me?

I had to ask.

"So," I began, as we headed towards the garden's exit. "I heard about *First Down*. Congrats!"

He jerked my arm and whipped me around to face him. His eyes narrowed and his normally friendly voice grew menacing as he squeezed my wrist. "What are you talking about?"

CHAPTER 18

"Ow! That hurts!"

"How do you know about *First Down*, Dani?"

"I don't even know what I'm talking about," I backtracked. "It's nothing—"

"You better not know anything," he growled.

"I don't," I sputtered, suddenly scared of this change in Nick. Gone was the caring, loving, boyfriend-to-be. Who the heck was this guy?

He spun around. "You do know! I thought you'd just back off, but no, you had to keep snooping."

Snooping?

"I didn't do anything," I squeaked, trying to step away from him, but his grasp was too tight.

"You had to keep snooping," he repeated, a crazed look darkening his eyes. "I figured switching your takeout box would do the trick, but you only seemed more intent on figuring it out."

"What are you talking about?"

Nick laughed like a madman. "I had a regular Pad Thai. All I had to do was write your name on my box, and poof!"

"Peanuts?" I gasped, unable to believe my own ears.

"I didn't mean for you to go to the hospital," he said, actually sounding sorry. But just for a second. "I just wanted to scare you, so you'd get the hell out of my way."

"I don't know what—"

"You just wouldn't leave well enough alone. Now *I* can't leave it alone." He lunged towards me, grabbing a handful of my hair and nearly ripping it out at the roots.

I screamed as I struggled out of his strong grip. I had to get out of there. I dropped my purse, kicked off my high heels, and ran.

I couldn't believe it! Nick was behind the sabotage?

I didn't have time to contemplate this new development. I definitely didn't want to end up like the stereotypical stupid teenage girl in a horror movie, so I had to get out of there. I heard his feet pounding on the stones of the walkway, the sound growing louder as he closed in.

For the second time that night, I felt Nick's breath on my neck, only this time it repulsed me. I felt so betrayed. I just couldn't take it any longer, so I whipped around and, before he could react, lunged forward and karate-kicked him in the kneecap.

Nick collapsed to his knees. I took that opportunity to get as far away as I could. Unfortunately, this section of the gardens was nearly pitch black, so I couldn't see where I was going and tripped over a stone bench, hitting my head. Great time for my klutziness to come back.

Stay here, Dani. Stay here. You can't pass out.

I concentrated on maintaining consciousness while I tried to muster the strength to get up. The silence in the gardens was so deafening I was sure I was dead.

The fall must have killed me. I was obviously walking around heaven right now.

But the silence probably only lasted thirty seconds before I heard deep breathing and crazed laughter. Nick was back!

I lifted my head and saw that my dance partner was less than fifty feet from me. I had no clue what to do. There was nowhere to hide and he was blocking the exit, so I couldn't possibly get out of there. Without even thinking, I scrambled up to the lower branches of the nearest tree, scraping my legs on the rough bark. I could feel blood dripping down my leg, but I didn't have time to worry about that.

"Dani?" I saw him approach the tree, but apparently he hadn't seen my escape. "Dani? Where are you? We can talk about this."

He tried to kill me and now he wanted to talk? No freaking way.

"Dani? Are you there? I didn't mean to hurt you. Nobody was supposed to get hurt."

There was a long pause while he continued to search for me. I held my breath; I didn't want him to hear me.

"The bomb was just a joke. It was fake!"

I heard a rustling behind a tree off to my left, maybe twenty feet away. Apparently Nick heard it too, because he whipped around in that direction, but he didn't run. He stayed right in place, as if glued there.

"Dani? Please, let's talk."

He was right below me, so using the branch as an improvised gymnastics apparatus, I swung my legs out and kicked him as hard as I could in his chest. Guess all those *battements* during barre exercises were good for something. He fell to the ground with a cry.

I jumped down. I really wanted to just get the heck out of Dodge City, but I knew nobody would believe me, and he'd only try to hurt me again. So, like all those action heroine babes in Whitney's favorite movies, I had to finish him off.

I stood over him and stared into his eyes. What I saw staring back was pure, unadulterated hatred. Well, you know what? I wasn't exactly feeling any love for him, either. How could I have been so blind before?

I kicked him swiftly in the ribs, prompting him to scream. While he was distracted by the pain, I grabbed his limp arm, positioned my knee against his elbow, and pushed it until I heard a snap. He yelled out in pain. Thank God for those self-defense classes Mom made me take!

"That was for the peanuts, you asshole! You could've killed me!"

I looked down at him, huddled in the fetal position, clutching his arm and writhing in pain. I knew I'd broken it. Well, too bad. He wasn't going anywhere. I'd just find my purse, dig out my cell phone, and call for—

"Are you okay?"

Craig?

He stepped out of the shadows and tentatively placed his arms around my shoulders. As pissed as I was that he'd stood me up for our coffee date, I had to admit the tingles I felt right then were a thousand times more powerful than when Nick touched me.

No, make that a million times.

What's that all about? Has to be the adrenalin rush.

"What the heck are you doing here?" I whispered.

"Bev saw me in the hallway and said you were in trouble."

"Bev?"

I was so confused by the turn of events that I didn't even notice the flashlights sneaking up on us.

I forced out a laugh as the officers swarmed the scene. "What took you so long?"

"I still don't understand how the police knew to come," I said the next day, surrounded by my own little Scooby Gang.

Whitney (hey, she promised she wouldn't tell Mom and Dad if I let her come visit and introduced her to JMC) laughed. "You never hung up the phone, you ditz. I heard him threaten you, so I called your room and spoke to Bev."

"And I called the cops." Bev cracked her knuckles. "Good thing you wanted to brag about your first kiss."

"It wasn't my first kiss," I grumbled, praying my face wouldn't turn bright red.

Analisa slowly shook her head. "Such a waste of talent. Nick was so intent on filming *First Down* that he was willing to sabotage the show to get out of his TV contract."

"That's crazy," Tim said.

JMC raked his fingers through his hair. "What a loser. I don't know why I ever hung out with him."

"And the ironic thing?" Maya said. "The movie producer was counting on Nick's appearance on *Teen Celebrity Dance-Off* to bring attention to the film."

"Nick thought he had to be available right now, but they're not planning to start filming for another few months," Analisa added.

"And now he won't even be able to do that," I said. "He's going to be in jail for a very long time. Arson and assault are serious crimes. I found the hacksaw he used to cut the tie-downs and the police say his fingerprints were all over it."

Bev nodded. "It's just a matter of time before they connect him to the fire, too."

"I'd be happy to step into his role in the movie," Craig volunteered, a sly grin on his face.

"I'm pretty sure nobody asked you," Maya said dryly, although I detected a hint of laughter in her eyes.

Craig picked up a pillow and clutched it to his chest dramatically. "You're breaking my heart!"

"Actually, Craig *is* gonna be in the movie," I said.

"What do you mean?" Kyle asked.

Craig shrugged. "I auditioned for a small role two weeks ago."

"You know, when he stood me up," I added. "He was actually out in Hollywood."

"I just got a call from my agent this afternoon." He smiled, once again revealing those killer dimples. "I got the part!"

"Oh my gosh!"

"That's awesome!"

"Dude, why were you holding out on us?"

Craig beamed. "Thanks guys. They just need to recast the lead, and then we start filming after Christmas."

Maya reached out and placed her hand on Craig's shoulder. "I think I owe you an apology."

"What for?"

"I told Dani she shouldn't waste her time with you." She hung her head, probably the first time I'd ever seen her look so contrite. "And I also thought you were behind the sabotage."

"Actually, we all did," I admitted.

He laughed. "I know you did. I told Kyle that petition was a stupid idea." He playfully swatted at the back of his friend's head.

"Don't look at me, dude." Kyle raised his hands in protest. "You wanted to get on that show, too."

"We thought you were trying to get Dani kicked off the show so Hadley would win," Analisa explained.

"Hadley?" Craig burst out laughing. "Why would I want that snob to win?"

"But I thought—"

Craig shook his head. "We broke up during the summer."

"So, you're not together?"

"I'm totally single." A smile broke out across his face. "Man, no wonder you suspected me. I didn't think I could convince you, so I decided to do some investigating on my own and help you out."

"Wait a sec, were you the face in the window?" I asked, mentally putting things together.

"The what?"

"I saw a face in the window of the dance studio one day. I thought it might be the saboteur."

Craig laughed. "Yeah, that was probably me. Guess I'm not cut out for covert work."

"So what are they doing about the show?" Whitney asked, sneaking a look at JMC.

"They cancelled it, but the producers are gonna let us perform live next Sunday night," I explained. "It's too late to schedule something else for that time slot, so they're doing a showcase of the school's talent, along with the stars from the show."

"Yeah," Ryan piped up. "My band's gonna play."

Craig nodded. "I'm doing a scene from *Streetcar Named Desire* and also that jive routine with Dani."

I nodded. "As long as I agree to go to nutrition counseling and get some help, the school will let me be on the show."

"And now that we won't be tied up with the show all semester, we've got time to audition for *Nutcracker*," Maya said.

"So we all win in the end," Analisa agreed.

I smirked. "Except for Nick."

Everyone laughed, and I tentatively scooched up closer to Craig. His arm fell lightly onto my shoulders.

Interesting ... Very interesting.

But I couldn't think about that right now. I had a TV show to prepare for.

DANCE GLOSSARY

Can you tell the difference between a *relevé* and a *rumba*? A *pirouette* and a *paso doble*? A *fouetté* and a *foxtrot*?

Dani and her friends have been dancing for years, so the ballet terms are pretty much a second language for them. Even still, they are just learning the ballroom lingo. For the rest of us, here's a cheat sheet.

À la seconde –To the side or in the second position. *À la seconde* usually means a step that moves sideways or a movement done to the side such as *grand battement à la seconde*.

Adage; adagio — In song, "adagio" means "slowly", and in ballet it means slow, enfolding movements. In a classical ballet class, the Adagio portion of the lesson concentrates on slow movements to improve the dancer's ability to control the leg and increase extension (i.e., to bring the leg into high positions with control and ease). In a *Grand Pas* (or Classical *Pas de deux, Grand Pas d'action*, etc.), the Adagio is usually referred to as the Grand adage, and often follows the Entrée. This Adage is typically the outward movement of the Grand Pas where the female dancer is partnered by the lead male dancer and/or one or more suitors. In ballet, the word adagio does not refer to the music accompanying the dance but rather the type of balletic movement being performed.

American Style — This term describes a particular style of ballroom dance developed in the United States that contrasts with the International Style. It denotes the group of dances danced in American Style ballroom competitions, consisting of two categories: American Smooth and American Rhythm.

Allegro — A term applied to all bright, fast, or brisk movements. All steps of elevation such as the entrechat, cabriole, assemblé, jeté and so on, come under this classification. The majority of dances, both solo and group, are built on allegro. The most important qualities to aim at in allégro are lightness, smoothness and ballon.

Arabesque — A pose in which the dancer stands on one leg, with the other leg lifted and extended to the back.

Arriere — French for "back" or "backwards," opposed to *avant*. A step *en arrière* moves backwards, away from the audience.

Assemblée — A movement where the first foot performs a swishing out, with the dancer launching into a jump. The second foot then swishes up under the first foot. The feet meet together in mid-air, and the dancer lands with both feet on the floor at the same time.

Attitude — A pose in which the dancer stands on one leg, with the other leg lifted and the knee bent at approximately 120-degree angle. The lifted or working leg can be behind (*derrière*), in front (*devant*), or on the side (*à la seconde*) of the body.

Avant — "Forward", to the front, as opposed to **arrière**. For example, a step travelling *en avant* moves forwards towards the audience.

Ballerina — Italian word for "female dancer," this term usually refers to the principal female dancer of a ballet company. Term is used in both Italian and English.

Ballerino — Italian word for "male dancer," this term is not used in English.

Barre — Horizontal bar, approximately waist height, used for warm-up and exercises for ballet techniques. Barre work usually takes up to the first half of each class. Warm up exercises may sometimes include stretching and various ballet positions that relax a ballerina's muscles. The study of ballet, and each class, will commonly start at the barre for everyone. Usually wooden or metal and mounted along a wall, often with the mirrors, there are also portable barres for individuals or group work.

Battement — Kicking the leg as high as possible into the air.

Brisé — A jump in which one leg is thrust from the fifth position to the second position in the air; the second leg reaches the first in mid-air executing a beat.

Bolero — Originally a Spanish dance in 3/4 time, the Bolero was modified in Cuba to become 2/4 time, and then eventually into 4/4. It is part of the American Rhythm syllabus.

Boureé — Small, quick steps usually done on the toes. In ballet it is used to describe quick, even movements often done en pointe; the movement gives the look of gliding.

Changement — A jump in which the feet change positions in the air.

Chaîné — A series of short, quick turns on pointe by which a dancer moves across the stage.

Cha-cha — The most recently developed of the Latin dances, it is usually danced to music with a tempo in the range of 110-130 beats per minute.

Fouetté — A turn with a quick change in the direction of the working leg as it passes in front of or behind the supporting leg.

Foxtrot — One of the five "standard" ballroom dances, typically danced to Big Band-style music written in 4/4 time. Foxtrot appears in both the American-style and International-style syllabi.

Jive — One of the five Latin competition dances, this is a fast tempo triple-step swing dance made popular during WWII by the swing music of Benny Goodman, Tommy Dorsey, and Glen Miller.

Partnering — Effort by both the male and female dancers to achieve a harmony of movement. Also known as *pas de deux*, dance for two.

Paso doble — A moderately fast Spanish bullfighter's dance. The music, set in march time, is often played at bullfights.

Petit allegro — Quick tempo dance steps characterized by lots of jumps and small movements.

Pirouette — A complete turn on one leg, usually going around more than once. The dancer must "spot" in order to avoid becoming disoriented.

Plié — A smooth and continuous bending of the knees.

Pointe — In ballet, dancing that is performed on the tips of the toes. Ballerinas wear special pointe shoes when doing pointe work.

Quickstep — Very fast and lively Standard dance, comprised of hops, kicks, and skips. Began as a faster version of the foxtrot mixed with the Charleston, with jazz influences.

Rock step — Two weight changes with the feet apart, taken in any direction.

Rumba — A slow, sensuous romantic Latin dance spotlighting the lady and featuring flirtatious interaction between the partners. Referred to as "the dance of love."

Samba — The official dance of Brazil, this Latin dance has a tempo of about 100 beats per minute.

Spotting — A periodic whipping of the head, in which a dancer keeps her gaze on a single spot. Dancers "spot" so that they will be able to turn without getting dizzy.

Tango — One of the five "standard" ballroom dances, characterized by sharp head-turns and provocative footwork.

Triple step — A three-step sequence taken on two beats of music, popular in swing and jive.

Waltz — The most popular ballroom dance in the world, the waltz has a slow and easy three-count rhythm, and can be danced to music found in nearly all genres.

Viennese Waltz — Fast waltz originated in Austria. The music is fast in tempo and sends the couple swirling around the ballroom

**Dani's next adventure starts
in May 2012!**

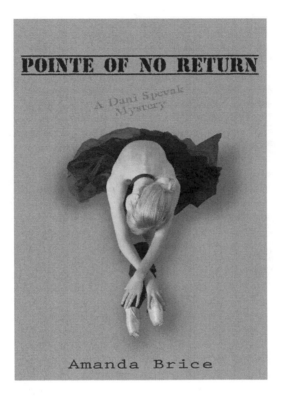

When her nemesis Hadley mysteriously disappears, Dani is assigned to dance her role in the *The Nutcracker*. But something doesn't feel right, so Dani decides to investigate, even if it means she won't get to perform. Will she find Hadley before the curtain rises?

ABOUT THE AUTHOR

Photo © Alicia Chevalier

As a little girl, Amanda Brice dreamed of being either a ballerina or the author of a mystery series featuring a cool crime-solving chick named Nancy Flew, but her father urged her to "do something practical," so she went to law school and spent her days writing briefs and pleadings instead of fiction.

But dance and writing have remained a part of her life. Amanda was in a local dance company as a teen, and was a member of the ballroom dance team at Duke University, and continues this interest by her obsession with *Dancing with the Stars*, so it was only natural to set a teen mystery series at a dance school.

Amanda is the President of Washington Romance Writers, and is a two-time finalist for Romance Writers of America's Golden Heart® Award. She blogs every other Wednesday with the Fictionistas and every other Friday with Killer Fiction.

In her spare time, Amanda enjoys dancing, reading, cooking, traveling, and obsessing over whether Duke will beat Carolina in basketball. Go Devils!

You can learn more about Amanda and her books at www.amandabrice.net. And while you're there, drop her a line – Amanda loves hearing from readers!

15432366R00089

Made in the USA
Middletown, DE
04 November 2014